MORGAN LIMA

The Qualms of the Left Behind

a novel

Cover design by Ives Salbert.

Second edition

ISBN: 978-0-578-79317-7

This book was professionally typeset on Reedsy.
Find out more at reedsy.com

For Mom, Brennan, and Jonathan with all my love.

Prologue

The door was unlocked, so Alice let herself in. She tiptoed up the stairs so as not to wake Mary in case she was sleeping. According to Rory, she had been in and out of a hazy slumber for a few days now.

"Alice? Is that you?" she heard as she reached the landing.

"In the flesh," Alice replied, and she rounded the corner into the bedroom. The sight of her long-time friend stopped her abruptly in her tracks. There had been times in Alice's life where she was at the store and saw her grandmother bagging groceries. Only it wasn't her grandmother, because her grandmother lived in Sussex and she was in London. Also, her grandmother was bedridden at the time with a nasty bout of pneumonia. But the woman looked so like her relative and the only reason she knew it wasn't her was because of the place she was in at that moment. Seeing Mary now reminded her of that.

Mary was covered up to her chin by her duvet. Her face was pale and drained, and the whites of her eyes were now a distinguished yellow. Her beautiful eyes had lost their light and were now more grey than blue.

"Hello, stranger," she whispered weakly from the bed. She smiled at her friend, and Alice pulled up the rocking chair to the side of the bed. Mary wriggled her arm out from under the linens and held it out as an invitation for Alice to hold it. Alice took her hand, cold and clammy as it was, and absentmindedly stroked it with her thumb.

"Thank you for coming all the way to Abergele," Mary managed.

"I know it's not the easiest journey from London."

"That's alright," Alice waved her away.

Mary smiled. "Alice, there's a reason I asked you to come while Rory was out. He's meeting our lawyer about something, and it's the first time he's left my bedside for a week. So I have to be quick, and you have to listen to what I tell you."

"Of course." Alice was intrigued. When she first received Mary's hoarse message on her mobile asking her to visit, she only knew it could mean she was deteriorating. But her friend was not one for "last goodbyes." Or so Alice thought.

Mary took a shuddering breath. Her eyes were wide and pleading.

"Alice, I'm scared."

Alice increased the pressure with which she held Mary's hand.

"I'm not scared about dying," Mary continued, shaking her head vigorously. "I've known this was coming for a while. I knew even before they told me the drug wasn't working for me like it was other patients in the trial."

Alice nodded. "Then what's bothering you?"

Mary's eyes were shining. "Death is something that happens to everyone because it's a part of the deal. We have to die before we can experience real life with God, Alice. And I know that you and I don't agree on that. I know that you think that religion is ridiculous or whatever, but I know what I believe to be true. I'm not scared of dying because I know where I'm going. I know that I won't be hurting any more. But Rory will. Not only that, but I'm afraid that once I am gone, Rory won't have anything to live for."

Alice sat up straighter. Mary continued before she could interrupt. "I know that sounds narcissistic, believe me. But you've seen him. I have always lived my life knowing God would save me from my sickness, whether that be while alive or dead. But Rory lives for me. Once I am gone, I don't know what's going to happen to him."

Alice stared blankly at Mary. She was at a loss. Mary was rarely outspoken about her faith like this, but she never doubted it was an essential part of her life. But there was no way Alice could argue with Mary when she said that Rory idolized her. She knew that Mary was right. Once she died, Rory would see no point of the world. Because to Rory, Mary was his world.

"So what do we do?" she asked.

"I'm not going to ask you to try to convert him or anything," Mary half-laughed. "I've been praying for a while that God would give me the words to say that would comfort Rory. This is what I came up with." She gestured to her bedside table. "Could you reach in that drawer for me and pull out the envelope?"

Alice opened the drawer and abstracted the bulging manila envelope.

"What is it?"

"I've written Rory something that I'm leaving in your capable hands to give him when the time presents itself. Not right away, you know. But once some time has passed, and it's clear that it's the right moment."

"How will I know it's the right moment?"

Mary gave her a knowing look. "You'll know."

Alice nodded. She slipped the envelope inside her coat. She swallowed nervously. "Mary, are you asking me to like, save his soul?"

Mary shook her head. "No, no, not at all. That's not up to you or me. I just…" She stopped for a moment to catch her breath. "I can't bear the thought of Rory dealing with the inevitable pain of losing something he believed so wholeheartedly in. He has never known the comfort of something so permanent that he knows will last even when he dies. So I'm leaving a bit of me behind."

Alice nodded again. Suddenly a lump had formed in her throat. She tried to clear it by coughing, but it would not dissipate. She swallowed several times before she could speak. "I should get going. I don't want to run into Rory on my way out. Awkward questions, you know, and I'm a rubbish liar."

Mary giggled. It was similar to her old, hearty laugh, but weaker.

Like a watered-down whiskey. "Go on then."

Alice gathered her bag and headed toward the door. When she reached the doorway, Mary's hushed voice stopped her in her tracks.

"Take care of our Rory, Alice."

Alice turned her head back only halfway so that Mary wouldn't see the tears that had already spilled over. "Course, Mare." She hurried down the stairs without another word.

One

Rory took his index finger and absentmindedly drew back the curtain to observe the bustle of River Street. Cars had lined up down the street due to the minimal parking in the Abels' driveway. The road itself hadn't been this busy for years. Rory wished there had been no cause for such a crowd. And not only because then he wouldn't be expected to greet every guest, shake their hand, and act as host to them. But also because then, he would have no need for the condolences they came bearing.

Mrs. Abel had selected Moonlight Sonata by Beethoven to serenade the guests as they entered, one of Mary's favourites. But Rory didn't even notice. Of the dozens of people he could see entering the house just a floor below, none of them were the two people he actually wanted to see. He wondered when the last time most of these people had actually spoken to Mary was. He didn't recognize half of the guests. He guessed that was the point of the reception following a funeral. You showed up long enough to drop off food and a kind word that won't really help the situation that presented itself. Then you feel good about yourself because you think you have helped the ones who are hurting. But in reality, they are still left with the same hole in their heart that was there long before the shepherd's pie was consumed.

This was the way Rory's thoughts were leading, when a familiar voice drew him out of his reverie.

"Love, you can greet the guests at the door with us if you like. If you're ready to come downstairs, that is."

Rory knew that Mrs. Abel, Mary's mother, meant to be inclusive and comforting. But Rory wasn't sure if he would ever feel ready to go downstairs. He could stay up here, in Mary's childhood bedroom, forever. This was the way she had left it before she moved to Wales.

Before her condition had declined. Before she died.

The Abels had left her room the way it had been, perhaps not realizing that, even if Mary ever did come back to live with them, her interests would have changed drastically. She would have no longer wanted the posters of Radiohead, Prince Harry, or Orlando Bloom plaguing her wall. Rory supposed she would have kept the postcards she collected from travel books though. As well as the little black book residing on her nightstand, worn out from years of highlighting, annotating, and dog-earing. Even the gold words engraved on the front, Holy Bible, were faded slightly. Rory could hear the echo of Mary's voice, telling him, "The best news you'll ever hear, Rory. And it's written down in a book that more than half the world's population probably owns. It's in plain sight! And yet, we are such an unhappy species."

Rory never understood what Mary meant by this, and was frankly always too scared to ask. The only news he wanted to hear at this point was that all of this was a terrible nightmare. That he was in a coma and was going to wake up. Mary would be exhausted but awake by his bedside, holding his hand. Because then she would be alive instead of in a casket underground.

The postcards and Bible were all timeless to Mary, and not something to be thought of as a phase for her. Still, the pink wallpaper would have been something Mary would have hated by now. She couldn't stand anything pink since having to take medicine of the same color, which was prescribed to her when she became sick with a terrible stomach illness. Rory remembered never to get her pink flowers after that because the color repulsed her. Gradually, although it felt like an instant, Mary had drifted from her paisley skirts and brightly colored cardigans to skinny black jeans and purple trainers. Not that this change necessarily bothered Rory. He didn't care what she wore. It was the personality behind the skirts and jumpers that made him fall in love with her. Once that was taken away, what was left was not quite as captivating.

Unfortunately, Rory knew all about having the life swept out of you.

"Rory, dear?" Mrs. Abel's voice startled Rory. He had not been very attentive lately, and it had been hard for him to focus on anything. He had agreed to help the Abels, though, because he knew no matter how difficult this was for him, it was more difficult for them by a tenfold.

"Hm?" was Rory's reply. "Oh, yeah, of course, I'll come down." He took one last glance out the window. He turned and took Mrs. Abel's hand and made his way down the stairs, even though there were a thousand things he would rather do than greet the mourners. Such as jumping out of said window.

Mrs. Abel clung to Rory's arm with her other hand. She was a strong woman. She had to be, given the fateful life she was challenged with when she was just figuring out the whole parenting thing. Mary was a surprise to both her and Mr.

Abel. Not that they weren't prepared for a child; they simply weren't expecting such a lifestyle change two months after being married. She was a nervous wreck from day one. She obsessed over reading every parenting and birthing volume she could find at the local bookstore she and her husband owned. She didn't sleep for six months after Mary was born, for fear of the infant rolling over and suffocating in her sleep. Mr. Abel, while not the complete opposite of his spouse, was not quite as hands-on. He loved Mary dearly, but only skimmed the chapters that didn't have to do with the paternal aspect of parenting a child. They both worked hard and saved every penny they had, even when Mary was an infant. They wanted to ensure their baby girl was the brightest pupil when she got older and received the best education so she could have a bright and fruitful future. But when Mary turned five, her education fund slowly depleted as it began to fund her medical expenses. The healthcare itself may have been free, but the extra services and trips to hospitals and specialists all over the country proved to be quite expensive.

Hodgkin's lymphoma was not a term the Abels had ever heard before. However, being bookstore owners, they quickly read up on the cancer and researched everything that had yet been discovered about it. They also quickly discovered that you can know everything there is to know about an illness, but that doesn't mean you can cure it.

The Abels were always strong for Mary, never letting her cancer define who she was. Their Christian faith had always dominated over any trial they encountered. However, Mrs. Abel's strength was wavering these days. Her grip on Rory's arm told him that he'd have to hold it together for her just a few hours longer. Then he could let go everything he had been holding in since they stepped into the church for the funeral that morning.

The two of them entered the living room to find that many of the guests had already been let in by Mr. Abel, who was standing at the door by himself. They were eating the starters Mrs. Abel had spent all night making. Rory told her she didn't need to labour so much over them. That the guests would bring plenty of food. He would know. He and Mary had been to several of these. Mrs. Abel had insisted that the cooking was therapeutic to her and that she needed to keep busy. The hosts had also invested in good quality champagne and wine to serve, which the guests were happily consuming.

"See here," observed Mrs. Abel. "Everything seems to be going well, doesn't it? It turned out just like I wanted."

Wouldn't you have wanted Mary here too? Rory wondered but did not ask. He knew better. Mrs. Abel was trying to make everything perfect to honour Mary; he understood that. Pretending that everything was fine was Mrs. Abel's way of mourning. He was just tired of acting like he wasn't his old, acrimonious self.

The two of them approached Mr. Abel, who put his arm around his wife's waist and kissed her cheek. She turned the corners of her lips upward. It wasn't a smile. It was a mechanical maneuver, something that had become almost a reflex by now.

One of the guests entered through the doorway, someone Rory had never seen before in his life.

"It was a lovely service, Eliza," the woman said, offering Mrs. Abel a hug.

"Oh, thank you for coming, dear," Mrs. Abel replied.

"Mary would have appreciated you being here," Mr. Abel said.

"And you must be the boyfriend," the stranger said. "Russell, isn't it?"

"It's Rory," Rory said, trying to disguise his dismay.

"And I was her husband."

"Yes, well, we were glad to hear at least our Mary wasn't alone when she…passed," the woman continued.

Rory stared at the woman. How was he supposed to handle all these people like this one, calling Mary, his Mary, their own, when he had never even heard a mention of their names before? And it seemed like the predicament was mutual. Hardly any of the guests seemed to know who he was. Not that Rory cared, but this was not the ideal setting Rory had in mind to learn the names of all of Mary's relatives and family friends. He had imagined a gathering a bit less…somber.

"Thank you for coming," Rory replied, hiding his inexplicable rage toward this woman behind a tender handshake.

After the woman went inside, Rory turned to the Abels.

"I think I need some air if that's alright," he said.

"Of course, son," replied Mr. Abel. "Take as much time as you need. We know this is all a bit…overwhelming."

Rory nodded curtly and trotted down the front steps of the house. He took off down the sidewalk, not sure where he was headed. He stared at his feet as he walked. A random thought suddenly popped into his head as he counted his steps: one, two, one, two. How many more steps did he have in his lifetime? Were they numbered, just like his heartbeats? Just like everyone's? He looked up from his feet and shook his head, trying to clear it by closing his eyes. When he opened them, he was staring at a familiar face coming toward him.

"It's the little brother himself, then, is it?" Dex was always known for having perfect timing. His older brother was the only one who ever got him out of his head. Who distracted him from his own thoughts, who kept him from being his own worst enemy. Rory exhaled a breath of relief that he didn't realize he had been holding.

"Dex," Rory whispered.

Dex was wearing a black suit that almost identically matched his jet black hair. Probably the same one he wears to interviews, Rory thought. The sun, which hadn't made an appearance for several days, decided to make its debut specifically to reflect off Dex's green eyes, which squinted as he grinned at Rory coming toward him.

Since completing medical school at Hull York, Dex had interviewed at numerous different hospitals, eventually landing on one right in the middle of London, making his dream of living in the city as a physician come full circle. Or it would, once he completed his student training.

Dex and the young woman trailing behind him caught up to Rory, and Dex pulled his little brother to his chest in a firm embrace. Dex's broad shoulders engulfed Rory's slight figure. The two brothers, close as they were, looked nearly nothing alike. While Dex towered over everyone in any given room, Rory's short stature hardly got him noticed. Dex's hair was that of what girls would always refer to as a "sex god," whereas Rory's thin wisps of hair aged him much more than he would have liked it to. Rory never could seem to keep up with Dex.

Not with looks, with academics, with health...

"Glad to see me too, then?" Dex's girlfriend, whom Rory had known longer than Dex had, pulled Rory into an embrace as well. She let go and held him at arms' length, her expression growing somber. Rory almost wouldn't have recognized her from far away if she hadn't been pinned to Dex's side. For one, Alice never wore heels. And her auburn hair was usually a mess of waves covering her face, not pulled up in a tight bun as it was today. "Rory, I am so sorry."

"Cheers, Alice," Rory said. He looked over her head, which he had been able to do since they were kids. Short though he was, he was still at least a head taller than Alice.

"Haven't told Mum and Dad yet, then?" Rory asked, with a tone that suggested he didn't actually care whether his parents had accompanied his brother.

"Actually, I called them last Tuesday," Dex replied hesitantly. "I told them the Abels' address, but they sounded like they already had plans."

"Yeah, plans to uphold their promise to never speak to me regarding Mary as long as I live," Rory spat, unable to hide his resentment any longer. "I guess the demise of the relationship causing that unspoken contract to come into agreement in the first place doesn't meet the requirements of its dissolution."

"Rory, don't," Alice said reproachfully. "Today is not the day."

"I can act however I like," Rory retorted. "I feel like I've earned that right. I buried the woman I love today, so you'll excuse me if I'm a bit spiteful toward the only two people in the world who hated her."

"Fair enough then," Alice responded. She knew by now when there was no reasoning with Rory, and this was not the battle she would choose to fight.

Dex looked at Rory with a sense of urgency.

"Rory, look, we should have come sooner," he began, but Rory shook his head.

"No, listen," Dex continued. "We really should have come to see you. It's just Alice has been busy with work, and I haven't been able to find enough people to cover my shifts. But look, we're taking you back with us, alright? No arguments."

Rory looked up at him in confusion. Was this the only reason they had come all the way to York? They thought he was incapable of carrying on with his life without a woman in it? They felt that they could just pick him up from his home and move him to wherever it was convenient for them?

"What, you think since I haven't got Mary around anymore I can just pick up my life and move it somewhere else?" Rory said defensively. "You think just because the love of my life is dead, and never coming back, that I don't have plans? I don't need you or Alice. I don't want your pity."

The truth was, Rory did have plans. Well, a plan. And it didn't involve his brother or his brother's girlfriend. Or anyone, for that matter.

Alice, who was in rare form, responded softly.

"I know that it's going to take a while, Rory, but we're going to help you pick up the pieces of your life and put them back together."

"Mary was my life!" Rory shouted. He knew he was breaking. He hadn't intended to lose it before the wake was over; he needed to gather control.

Dex put his arm around his brother, and the three of them began to walk toward the house.

"I know she was, mate," he said consolingly. "That's also why I know you have made no plans whatsoever to get on with it."

Rory looked down. "And how exactly am I supposed to do that?"

"Let us take you back to London with us," Dex offered. "I know you always said you hated the city, but you hate everything, so I'm in no mood to try and negotiate with you. I know that you had to move out of your cottage in Abergele. And I know you're not ready to let Mum and Dad help you. So let us. We have an extra room, and

Alice already set it up for you."

Alice offered one of her friendly smiles that she reserved only for Rory when he was down. Actually down, not just when he was in one of his usual bad moods. But Rory couldn't take Dex up on his offer.

"Look," Rory said, "the Abels really need my help around the house. They're grieving, and I've been doing most of the upkeep."

"Yes," Alice said, "but have you had any time to grieve for yourself?"

"Wait," Rory said, holding up his hand. "You two want to keep me on suicide watch, is that it?" He was not going to let the two of them interfere with his plan.

"Why would we waste our time?" Dex asked. "There'd be no point, you're already a dead man walking." He cracked a smile.

The corners of Rory's mouth turned up before he could stop them, but unlike Mrs. Abel's mechanical smile, this slight grin was genuine. There were only two people in the world who were allowed to joke about Rory's illness besides himself and Mary. And they were standing right there next to him.

Mrs. Abel's voice called from the front steps. "Rory! I need your help, please."

"I'll be right there, Mrs. Abel," Rory called back to her. He turned to Dex and Alice. "I'll think about it."

"Great, so we'll start moving you in then," Alice chirped.

"Are you not hearing me?" Rory replied.

"Oh, I'm hearing you. I'm just choosing not to listen." Alice smiled her usual grin at him, revealing the gap in her two front teeth. She had always been so embarrassed about it growing up, but it was Rory who had convinced her not to get it fixed.

'For just two teeth?' he had cried. "Just leave them, they make you Alice." She never complained about it again.

Rory ran ahead of his two visitors and up the front steps to see what Mrs. Abel's requests were.

"Oh good, Rory, there you are," sighed Mrs. Abel when she saw him. She was carrying two empty plates loaded with cutlery while balancing three empty wine glasses in her other hand. "Could you just nick that glass of wine from Mark's mother? It's her fifth glass, I'm afraid, and if I try, I am certain she will try to slap me."

"Sure, anything, Mrs. Abel." Rory made his way over to Mr. Abel's mother, who was sitting on the couch, talking to no one in particular quite tearfully about how the elderly should never outlive the young. Wine was spilling out of her glass every time she made a dramatic gesture. "Grandma Abel?"

The woman looked up, surprised that someone was addressing her.

"Oh, um, hello," the old woman began. "Oh, dear, I'm so sorry. I know you were a friend of Mary's, but I seem to have forgotten
your name."

Rory was slightly disappointed. This was a family member he actually knew and had hoped she would have remembered him.

"It's Rory, Grandma," Rory reminded her.

"Oh, yes!" the woman exclaimed. "Rory! So good to see you again, dear. Of course, under the most dreadful circumstances." She glanced around at the sea of people. Some were reminiscing, some were crying, and a few were children, running about, seemingly clueless as to where they were. Rory hated the kids the least of the lot.

15

"Yes, well, I'm collecting glasses so if I could just have yours?" Rory reached for her glass, but Mary's grandmother swayed her arm away from his reach.

"Wait a minute," she began again. "I think I remember my son telling me that you were there when my sweet Mary died. Is this true?" Rory wished people would stop bringing this up. "Er, yes this is true," Rory responded impatiently.

"What was the last thing she said?" Grandma asked, her eyes welling up with tears. "Did she mention any of us?" She indicated the family in the living room. "Perhaps me?"

Rory was extremely uncomfortable, and was in no mood to entertain the questions of a drunk eighty-year-old woman. "Uh, no," Rory said. "In the end, she went pretty quietly and peacefully...Your glass, please, Grandma." But the infuriating woman would not relinquish her crystal.

She continued, "Yes, well, I suppose that's for the best. Forgive me, dear, but my memory isn't quite what it used to be. You were her...good friend, yes?"

Rory's heart sank. "We were married, Grandma Abel, remember? You sent us the lovely china set as a wedding gift a few years ago."

"Oh!" the old woman exclaimed. "Yes, well, details tend to escape you as you get older. You will learn."

"If I'm lucky," Rory muttered, this time snatching her glass from her before she could realize what was happening. He moved on to clear the empty glasses in the dining room. As he bent over to place all the empty dishes on a plate, a voice startled him from behind.

"Here, mate, you can take this as well."

Rory whipped around to stare into the face of someone he was sure he had never met before, yet thought he had seen his face somewhere. He stared at the young man and his empty plate. Even though it did not register with Rory who this person was, the man definitely recognized Rory.

"Oh," he said. "You're the bloke who gave the eulogy at the service, weren't you?"

"Yeah," Rory replied. "Sorry, who are you?"

"Oh, sorry, mate," the man said. "I'm Alexander. I went to school with Mary when we were younger. Neighbours for years. My family moved away years ago, but I always missed her. I didn't know her illness had got so bad. I thought she was doing better since I hadn't heard from her."

"You didn't hear from her for years, so you assumed she was better?" Rory asked dully.

"Yeah, well, you know the saying. No news is good news, right?" Alexander said. "Anyway, I recently moved back. When I tried to make plans or contact Mary…that's when I found out. Dreadful, isn't it? The eulogy, by the way, was beautiful. I assume you were close to Mary?"

"We were married, actually," Rory said, not trying to hide how much he disliked this stranger who had forgotten about Mary.

"Oh!" Alexander said with surprise. "The Abels didn't mention."

"Perhaps because anybody who was close to Mary already knew," Rory responded.

Alexander paused, recognizing for the first time since beginning their conversation that Rory disliked him. Thinking he could salvage the situation and possibly redeem himself, he continued, "So how did you two meet? Uni? Mary always dreamt of going to Oxford.

Never found out how that turned out for her, though."

"We met at a support group for cancer victims here in York,"

Rory said.

"Oh," Alexander's plan of showing how he knew of Mary's hopes and dreams obviously backfiring on him. "Oh! So you mean...you too?" Alexander was suddenly obviously very uncomfortable.

"Don't worry," Rory reassured him sarcastically. "It's not contagious."

"No, it's not that, it's just..." Alexander had apparently run out of things to say.

"You can go," Rory told him.

"Right," said Alexander.

Rory watched as Alexander grabbed his jacket off the coat rack.

His muscles filled it out perfectly, Rory noticed with envy. He wasn't sure why Alexander was so familiar to him, and he had no intention of figuring it out.

Two

Dex pulled up to the front of the flat and put the rental car in park. He looked over at Rory, unable to tell if he was sleeping or just avoiding talking to him, as his eyes had been closed since Dex had collected him. They had stayed that way for the four-hour car ride as well. Still, Dex took the sign of Rory with his packed boxes and knapsack, sitting on the Abels' stoop, as a sign that there would be no struggle.

Dex studied Rory for a moment. He could remember when they were boys, and they would go on long car rides with their dad while their mum stayed home to tend to the shop they owned. Rory was always such a restless sleeper, tossing and turning the entire trip. He would jerk awake every half hour or so, and Dex would have to remind Rory where they were, that they were safe. As Rory got older, this habit didn't go away. But instead of comforting his brother, Dex would shove him and tell him to shut up, that he couldn't hear his music. As Dex stared at Rory now, he wondered at what age older siblings were supposed to stop consoling their younger siblings and start making them more resilient. Had Dex started too early? Was there even such a thing as too late?

"Ror, I know you're awake," Dex said, shaking off the familiar feeling of guilt he had whenever he was around his brother after not seeing him for months on end.

"Then you know why I'm pretending to sleep," replied Rory, his eyes still glued shut.

"Ror, we're here, and if you don't get out now, I'll make you sleep in the car."

"Ah, that's just my style though, isn't it?" Rory asked. "Go ahead then, I'll be fine." He adjusted the seat to that in reclined, making himself more comfortable.

"Go on then, but Alice has been working hard all day to make your room the way you'd like it. She found old photographs of all of us. She's been in a tizzy all day waiting for you." This tugged at Rory's conscience, and he opened his eyes begrudgingly. Dex had already opened his door and was unloading the boxes from the back. Rory grunted and got out of his seat, going around to help his brother.

It only took one trip for the two of them to carry all of Rory's belongings. He had given most of Mary's items back to the Abels, and only kept what he knew he couldn't live without: the bottle of perfume he bought her for her last birthday, her favorite jumper (which had initially been his, but she wore it so often it permanently smelled like her), and his favorite photograph of the two of them, framed. She was staring at the camera, taking the picture. Rory was standing behind her, his arms wrapped around her waist. He was smiling, but not into the lens. His smile fell into the side of her neck, his forehead resting on the side of hers.

When the two brothers reached the top of the stairs, Dex whispered to Rory, "Be kind, yeah?"

Rory acted affronted. "I'm always kind."

Dex stared at Rory pointedly.

"I'll try harder," Rory agreed.

Dex unlocked the door to the flat. They heard the clicking of heels before he even got the door open. Alice swung the door open wide and exclaimed, "Lovey!"

She kissed Dex and took the box he was carrying from him, lightening his load. She pulled Rory in and shut the door, grabbing his boxes and putting them on the floor as well. She flung her arms around her old friend, kissing him on the cheek.

"I am so glad you're here!" Alice gushed. "Was the drive here alright? No hiccups or anything?"

Rory couldn't believe this was the same girl with whom he used to ditch school and smoke spliffs behind the library. And now here she was standing in front of him wearing an apron and holding a wooden spoon, her hair pulled up in a tight knot at the base of her neck. Wearing heels.

"No hiccups," reassured Dex, as is gave her another kiss.

And here's Dex, Rory thought. His older brother who never paid any attention to the two of them before Rory got sick. Who was so consumed in studying for his medical examinations, determined not to inherit the unfortunate life of a bankrupt shop owner from their father.

"Good, that's really good," Alice said. "Dex, you can show Rory to his room, please, and I'll just finish up supper and get it on the

table."

"Right. Rory, follow me." Rory followed Dex through the living room and down the hall to Rory's new bedroom. When he first entered it, he wasn't sure whether he should be in awe or be angry that Alice had thought he would like the collage of memories that was plastered on an entire wall. But, nonetheless, there they were. Polaroid photographs with him and Mary, him

21

and Alice, and all four of the friends together. Rory stood in front of the wall for what seemed like an eternity until Dex pulled him out of his trance.

"Where do you want this, mate?" Dex was struggling to carry one of the larger boxes Rory had brought.

Rory whipped his head around. "I don't care."

Dex set it down next to the queen sized bed he had set up earlier that week. Alice had picked out the blue plaid quilt that draped across it.

"It's ready!" Alice's voice called from the kitchen.

The two men made their way to the dining room table, located just off the kitchen. Rory realized that for a primary school teacher and an F1 physician, these two sure were living it up in London.

Rory sat down and stared at his plate. Immediately he felt his stomach turn and felt hot liquid rise up into his mouth. Meat loaf and chips? He'd rather jump off a cliff. His medication for his treatment regularly made him feel nauseated.

"Tuck in, then," invited Alice, as she did so herself. "Sorry I didn't have much time to whip up anything fancy. Had a meeting after school today with one of the parents."

"Oh?" asked Dex. "How did it go?"

"Absolutely awful," Alice replied. "Her child is going to get thrown out if he can't contain himself. He likes to throw rocks. At everything."

Dex chuckled. Alice looked at Rory, noticing that he hadn't touched any of his food.

"You don't like meat loaf, Ror?" asked Alice, worriedly. "I thought it was your favorite."

Rory looked up at Alice, his mind a thousand miles away. It seemed to be that way a lot these days.

"Don't make a girl cry now, after the day I've had," said Alice jokingly. "Go ahead, try it. You might like it. Or hate it. Either way, it's sustenance."

"Sorry," Rory apologized. "It's just…I'm not hungry. It takes a lot for me to eat these days because everything just comes back up."

"Rory, you haven't eaten a thing all day," said Dex.

"That's because I don't want to be sick," said Rory.

"Well, you are sick," said Dex, losing his patience. "And that's why you've got to eat. Come on, you have to take your meds with food. You know that."

"You're not my doctor," said Rory, growing frustrated.

"I know I'm not your doctor," retorted Dex. "But I am *a* doctor.

And besides, I'm your brother."

"Oh, so that means I have to listen to you?" Rory was angry now.

He knew moving in with Dex would mean being watched like a hawk.

"What it means is that I know what's best for you," claimed Dex.

"No, it doesn't, because you're not my physician!"

"Rory, don't be ridiculous, you need to eat—-"

"Yes, but you're not my doctor, are you—-"

"Rory, stop yelling—-"

"I'm not YELLING!"

Silence settled upon the table. Alice was the first to attempt to break the awkwardness.

"Who is your GP then, Rory?" Alice asked.

Rory didn't take his eyes off of Dex. "Dr. Sylvester."

"No, that was your doctor back in Wales," Dex corrected him.

"Your new doctor is Dr. Epstein. He's agreed to take you on as a patient, given the circumstances. And the fact that he is a colleague didn't hurt. He's the best in the area, mind you."

"I suppose I should thank you for making this transition much easier for me," sneered Rory.

"I'm not looking for any sort of gratitude from you, Rory. But I won't let you sit here and insult Alice by not eating the meal she's cooked for you. It doesn't have to be like this, Ror. Us three living together, it could be fun. Like when we were kids."

"Oh, you mean before I met Mary?" said Rory. He looked down at his plate hesitantly and took a bit of his supper. "It's delicious, Alice."

"Cheers, Rory," Alice said softly.

Alice's voice was never soft. It always overtook everyone else's. It was a booming gawk of a voice, and Rory had silenced that. As Rory lay in his new room, staring up at the blank, white ceiling, he couldn't help but feel guilty. He seemed to be feeling a lot of that these days. He also felt like a stranger in this new place. The white ceilings were only the start of it. Mary had filled theirs in their home in Wales with her own paintings. Designs that mimicked a night's sky. They were stunning, and it gave both her and him something to appreciate through all those days they were bed bound.

However, what the ceilings lacked, the walls made up for. They were covered in posters of vintage advertisements, which were Alice's avocation. A single nightstand stood next to his bed, keeping it company. His luggage littered the floor, so Rory chose a random box and began unpacking it. He didn't get very far before he heard a knock on the door. It was Alice, holding a bottle of pills.

"I brought you these," she said. "Dex says you usually take them after supper. Your other meds are in the cabinet in the bathroom down the hall."

Rory took the bottle, opened it, and popped a single capsule in his mouth, swallowing it dry. "Rory," Alice continued, "I just want to say that I'm sorry."

"Mary dying isn't your fault, Alice," Rory said, returning to unpacking his box. "Nor is it anyone else's even though everyone seems to keep feeling obligated to apologize."

"No, I wasn't talking about Mary," said Alice. "I was talking about this."

Rory, bending over his box, looked up.

"What?" he asked.

"This!" exclaimed Alice. "This...awkward situation. I don't know what to say to you, Rory, which is weird for me. When have I ever not known what to say to you? Tonight, at supper? That's not how we talk. We're real with each other. And we never indulge in the bitterness, even though it's tempting. But you have every excuse to now, I know that. I just feel like I don't know how to be a good friend to you."

"You're doing fine, Alice," Rory muttered. He looked up, realizing how insincere he sounded. Alice wasn't the enemy here.

"Thank you for the room. I really do appreciate what you've done with it."

Alice looked around the room, smiling, clearly pleased with her work. She turned back to Rory.

"Don't worry about finding a job anytime soon," she said. "Dex and I can still pay the rent. It's not a problem."

"I'll find work," said Rory.

"Rory, you don't have to—-"

"I said I'll find something, okay?" Rory went back to unpacking.

Alice was taken aback. Ten years ago she would have picked this fight. But times had changed. So had they.

"School starts at eight for me." Alice's tone suddenly changed to businesslike. "So I need to leave the house by seven. Dex goes in to work around then too, so I usually put on a fresh pot of coffee for him. You're welcome to it as well as anything else in the kitchen.

I'll make breakfast tomorrow, and put it in the fridge. Just warm it up when you get hungry."

Rory didn't look up or indicate he had heard Alice. Giving up,

Alice turned on her heel to leave the room but stopped at the doorway. She looked back at her childhood friend, so much older and worn looking now.

"Goodnight, Ror," she said. And with that, Alice shut the door behind her. At the sound of the door closing, Rory looked up. He stared at the plain, wooden door for a moment, then went back to taking clothes out of the box and putting them in a dresser. He did this until the box was empty. Then he picked up the box and tore it to pieces.

Three

On the night table located right next to Rory's bed sat an alarm clock that Alice bought him. Not that it was of any use to Rory. He had nowhere to be. If it were up to him, he would have slept the day away. But at last, the birds squawking outside his window obviously had a different idea.

Rory woke up in a worse mood than he went to sleep in. He hadn't rested well at all, tossing and turning all night. Although his body was physically exhausted, his brain was working in overdrive. His subconscious haunted him with images of Mary. And when it wasn't taunting him with the 'what could have been,' he was hit with a blow when reality sunk in, and he knew she would never return to him.

After about an hour of debating whether to comply with the sun beckoning him to budge, Rory finally dragged himself out of bed to the kitchen. Again, he feared getting sick, so he was hesitant to heat up any of the omelet Alice had saved for him. In the end, he decided to go with dry toast and a cup of tea. The flat was empty. Dex and Alice had left for work hours ago. Rory thought for a split second about going out and getting a paper to see what job listings there were. Then he remembered how comfortable his bed had been, and decided to retreat back under his covers of solitude. He slept until Alice got home from work later that afternoon and came in his room to give him his meds. She made him sit at the table with her and Dex at supper, which, in Rory's opinion, basically went as well as the night before.

The days continued like this for the next couple of weeks. Rory had become accustomed to living in a daze that was induced by several of the meds he was taking. He was vaguely aware of the reservations

Alice and Dex had about his attitude, but in all honesty, he didn't care enough to address it. Not until the Night of the Overheard Conversation.

Rory had forgotten to take his meds after supper. Unfortunately for him, he realized this just as he was drifting off into a mind-numbing slumber. He debated whether it was worth it to get up, and not until he realized the sudden urge to go to the toilet did he make an effort to get out of bed.

As he finished washing his hands, he opened the medicine cabinet and searched through the five different pill bottles for the right one. He popped two tablets into his mouth and swallowed them dry. He flinched as they went down his throat and, shaking his head, started to make his way back to his bedroom. He stopped when he heard voices coming from Dex and Alice's bedroom, both of whom he thought were asleep. The door was cracked open, so he paused in the hallway to listen.

"It's just, it's been two weeks," Alice was saying.

"I know," Dex replied, "but it's going to take a lot longer than that for him to move on, Alice. It's Mary we're talking about, here."

"I just thought that maybe once he moved in with us and we

were able to remind him of the good old times it would at least help him along with the grieving process."

Alice's words hit Rory in the stomach. He felt his heart sinking.

"Rory isn't the same Rory we used to know," Dex said. "I don't know if he'll ever be the same person again. But we have to accept that and meet him where he's at."

And where exactly was that? Rory wondered. Alice was thinking along the same lines as him.

"And where is that?" she said. "I feel like don't even know him anymore."

"We're not teenagers now, Alice," Dex replied. "He's grown up. We all have. Even you," he chuckled.

"But it's like he doesn't even want our help," Alice continued seriously. "He's indifferent to us. And I'm…I'm worried what he might do."

"What he might do?" Dex asked, puzzled.

At that point, Rory shoved the door forward to reveal himself. Alice and Dex looked over at him simultaneously, surprised. They didn't know how much Rory had heard.

"Rory!" Dex tried to make light of the situation. "What's up, mate? Can't sleep?"

But all three of them knew the situation for what it truly was. Which is why Alice and Dex couldn't do anything but watch as Rory turned around and walked back to his room, slamming his door.

They were left staring into empty space.

What I might do? The words had confused Rory. He had never mentioned his plan, his way out, to anyone. He hadn't written it down. Was Alice on to him, or did she think he might have a psychotic break, and go all homicidal on her and Dex?

Rory tried to forget about the conversation, but he couldn't fall asleep. Obviously, his subconscious decided that reality, this time, was more torturous than teasing him with thoughts of his deceased love.

Rory was still awake when he heard Dex and Alice getting ready for work in the morning. He hadn't slept a wink that night. Apparently, the two other tenants had had the same problem falling asleep, because both of them had overslept and were running late.

Alice was bustling around the kitchen, shoveling Dex's medical papers, looking for her marked coloring pages.

"I have another meeting with a student's parents after school today so I won't be home until around six," said Alice as she stacked the coloring pages together and tucked them in her bag.

"I finish at six-thirty today, so just come to the office, and we'll catch the tube together," replied Dex.

"Really?" Alice was surprised. "Your boss is letting you off early again?"

"He knows about our situation," Dex nodded to Rory's bedroom door. The door may have been closed, but it wasn't soundproof. Rory knew he was talking about him.

"This will probably be the last time he lets me off early, though," Dex continued.

"That's brilliant!" said Alice, happy she was going to get to see Dex for more time than just when he stumbled in from working his double shift, as many F1 physicians had to, in the early hours of the morning.

Alice swung her bag over her shoulder and called out, "Rory, I put you a plate of leftovers in the fridge for when you get hungry! Dex and I will be home around seven."

Even though Rory heard her, he didn't make a sound. She hardly noticed, for at that moment she looked at her watch and saw the time.

"And, of course, I'm running late," she said exasperatedly. "Bye, Lovey." She turned to head out the door, but Dex reached out at the moment and grabbed her hand, spinning her into him.

"What—-" said Alice, but couldn't get the rest of sentence out because Dex was already giving her a deep kiss.

"Oh!" she said when it was over. "Maybe I should take you with me." She fumbled distractedly with his tie.

"I wish I could stick you in the pocket of my lab coat," Dex whispered in her ear.

"Mmm," Alice was entranced. But she quickly snapped out of it when she noticed her watch again. "Alright, now I really have to go." As she turned to leave, she looked behind her shoulder.

"Love you!" she called back to Dex, running out of the apartment before she could hear his response.

Dex shook his head at the sight of Alice dashing off, with her heels and frilly skirt, her bag swinging about. He went back to sorting his papers and put them in his briefcase. Just before he headed out the door, he stuck his head in Rory's room without knocking.

"Alice and I are gone, Ror. Don't forget to take your meds at noon. Be sure to take them with food. If you need anything, just call

Alice or me on one of our mobiles."

But Rory, who had heard Dex's footsteps, had turned on his side. He said nothing and kept his eyes shut tight. Dex always been able to tell when he was faking, though. He knew he was going to demand a response. But all Dex said was, "Alright then, Ror." And with that, he left his room. Rory waited until he heard the door to the flat shut. Then he turned over and stared at the digital alarm clock on his bedside, which read 07:42.

Rory must have fallen asleep, because the next time he looked at the clock, it said 18:47. Damn, Rory thought. He had slept through the day. He didn't even realize he had forgotten to take his meds. Even if he had, there is a good chance he wouldn't even have cared. He turned onto his back and stared at the ceiling. His mind was racing, and he tried his best to focus on only a single thought but was distracted by the dripping he heard coming from the bathroom faucet. No matter how hard he worked to block it out, the dripping was interrupting his thoughts. He slowly got up, feeling weak. Only then did he remember that he hadn't taken any meds that day. He groaned.

He sauntered to the bathroom in a daze. No matter how hard he tried, he couldn't clear his thoughts. When he reached the bathroom, he just stared at the dripping faucet for a few seconds before he suddenly slapped the tap down. He grabbed onto the sink with both hands, staring down into it. His heart was pounding, and he was having a hard time catching his breath. Suddenly his mind cleared and was able to focus on one, single thought. His quickly opened the cabinet and rummaged through the medicines and combs. He found the bottle of Fosamax, meant to strengthen his bones which had been worn down by radiation, and Morphine which was for the pain he felt after a day of working his muscles and bones to their maximum abilities. That, along with the Baclofen he took to relax his muscles, typically gave him enough relief for several hours before the burning sensation began again. He gathered all three bottles, closed the mirror, and looked down at his supplies. Finally, he lifted his head up to face his reflection and stared.

Dex held the door open for Alice, who was giving him a disapproving shake of the head. Dex, oblivious, continued with his story.

"You wouldn't have believed it if you saw it," he said impressively.

"Dex," Alice held up her hand to stop him from going on, "I don't want to hear about the world's largest cyst."

"I didn't say it was the world's largest cyst," corrected Dex. "Just the largest cyst our hospital has ever seen."

"Ugh," replied Alice, "I'm still not interested. What do you want for supper? We should've picked up a take-away, I'm so over this day." "Don't worry," said Dex, putting his arm around her as they entered the kitchen. "I'll cook us up something decent, just go check on Rory for me. He's probably slept the day away. I hope he remembered to take his meds, he didn't answer when I tried calling to remind him."

"Yeah, alright," said Alice, who wandered down the hall to Rory's bedroom while Dex started searching for ingredients he could put together to come up with a dish. When she reached his room, the door was cracked open, so she stuck her head in.

"Rory?" She peered around the door frame but saw no sign of him. She walked back to the kitchen.

"He's not in his room," she said to Dex.

"He's probably in the toilet," Dex replied.

Alice walked down the hall and found the door to the toilet was closed.

"You were right!" Alice called back to Dex. She knocked on the door. "Rory! What do you want for supper?" she called to him through the door.

There was no response from the other side.

"Rory," Alice continued, "I know you're in the loo, just tell me

33

what you want so Dex can get started. I'm starving, and I'm afraid if we don't make anything soon, I may resort to eating your only brother."

At that moment, Alice heard the sound of several pills scattering onto the tiled floor.

"Dammit!" came Rory's voice from behind the door.

Alice suddenly grew concerned and tried to open the door. It was locked.

"Rory?" She knocked several times. "Rory, what are you doing in there?" She heard Rory scrambling on the floor to pick up whatever he had dropped, and the sound of him beginning to hyperventilate.

Louder, and louder, more rapid breathing until it sounded as though he was gasping for air.

"Dex!" Alice screamed. "Dex, come here, now!"

At the sound of Alice's scream, he dropped the knife he was using to slice a tomato. He was halfway to the toilet before it even hit the kitchen tiles. He reached Alice in a matter of seconds.

"What's happened?" Dex demanded. "I think Rory's trying to do something," Alice cried frantically.

"I don't know what, but he won't let me in."

"Rory?" Dex called to him. "Stand back, Ror." Dex held the handle with his left hand and, with all the strength he could muster, shoved the door in, breaking through the lock. Slumped on the floor, leaning against the bathtub was Rory, looking defeated. His breathing was shallow and rapid. An open bottle of rubbing alcohol had spilled when he had accidentally knocked it over trying to pick up the pills, which were still all over the floor. When Rory saw that the two had got in, he scrambled to gather the tablets before they could.

"No!" Dex cried. He wasn't sure why, but instinct told him not to let Rory get his hands on the medicine. He grabbed his brother and pulled him back, which took little to no effort on Dex's part. Alice had begun to cry uncontrollably when she saw the scene, realizing what was happening. She grabbed the pills from Rory's hand and collected the others that had fallen on the floor while Dex restrained him.

"No!" Rory sobbed. "Stop it, just let me go! Let me GO!"

But Dex didn't release Rory. He held him close to his chest, his hands clutching Rory's arms to Rory's own chest, ensuring Rory wouldn't escape the embrace. Both of them fell backward onto the floor, Rory still sobbing. They stayed in this stance until Rory's breathing finally became more even. Alice sat down on the side of the tub, not daring to take her eyes off the scene of Dex and his brother. Once Rory had stopped fighting, she put her head in her hands and rubbed her eyes, seeing a swirl of colors through the darkness of shutting out her world.

Once Rory was calm enough, Dex helped him off the floor and led him to his room.

"Alice, get rid of the pills," Dex said over his shoulder. "We need to stop him from overdosing."

But Alice followed behind, still clutching the pills in her hand.

Dex sat Rory down on the foot of the bed and took a seat next to him. He put his arm around Rory and began to rub his shoulder affectionately. Rory simply stared straight ahead. Alice began to pace back and forth. When she could no longer stand the silence, she left. Rory didn't know where she had gone to, and he didn't care. And he wasn't about to acknowledge his brother's compassion. The two of them had ruined his plan. The only one he had. Well, that wasn't entirely true. It was the only plan he had left. Plan A was spending his life with his love.

Plan B was getting beaten by his cancer before Mary was. This had been Plan C. He didn't think he would need a Plan D.

Alice returned with a glass of water, but the pills were gone.

She had put them in a plastic bag and sealed it, leaving it in the kitchen.

She had counted the pills. Rory was unable to take any before she and Dex caught him.

Alice handed Rory the glass of water hesitantly, not sure if she should cry or yell at him. But all she said was, "What are you thinking,

Ror?"

Rory didn't look up. But he replied, "That I wouldn't have failed if these damn hands hadn't been shaking. Ironically due to all the drugs I'm taking for this bloody disease."

Alice didn't know what to say, so she silently took a seat on the other side of Rory, still holding the glass of water. The three of them sat in silence for what seemed like an eternity.

"Rory—-" Alice began, but Dex interrupted her.

"Alice, don't."

"What?" Alice looked at him.

"Say anything," Dex replied.

Alice was furious. "So you don't think we should address the fact that your brother just tried to kill himself with prescription meds and a bottle of rubbing alcohol?" she snapped.

Rory looked at her. "I'm dying, but I'm not deaf. Think of it as me just trying to speed this process along."

"That's not funny," said Alice coldly. "And you're not dying right now. You're just…not getting better. Anyway, you're not funny," she repeated. "Rory, just…how could you? How could you do this to

Dex and me?"

Rory didn't have a response. Not one that would make Alice feel any better, anyway.

"Well, I don't even know what to do now," Alice said, after several moments of the tension-building hush that had fallen over the room. "Dex? What do you think? Do we take him to the hospital? Do we call the paramedics?"

"No, Alice," Rory said urgently. "Please, you cannot call the paramedics. I didn't even take anything!"

"The psychiatric ward, then?" Alice said, her voice growing louder and slightly hysterical.

"If only you had come home one minute later," Rory said, burying his head in his hands.

"Then what?" Dex spoke for the first time since returning to the room. "Then we would have found you on the floor, foaming at the mouth? That's how you repay us? I don't care that you haven't made peace with Mum and Dad, but this is not how you treat the two people who care most about you in this world."

Alice suddenly got off the bed and stormed out, exasperated. Rory buried his head in his hands again, sobbing. Dex didn't know if he felt remorse or just more frustration at the unfortunate timing. Alice returned a few moments later, holding a long manila envelope tightly to her chest. She took a long look at her old friend, worn and crying. And at her boyfriend, who was no longer comforting his brother, but who was folding his arms across his chest, giving Alice a look that said, I'm at a loss here.

Alice nodded. She slowly approached Rory, forgetting her anger and franticness. She bent down in front of him and placed a hand on Rory's shoulder.

"Ror," she started. But Rory immediately jerked his shoulder back.

"Don't touch me!" he exclaimed. Alice exchanged a worried look with Dex.

"Rory," she tried again, "if you won't listen to me, then maybe you'll listen to Mary."

Rory slowly lifted his head from his hands and looked up at Alice. How dare she bring up Mary's name to him? He felt rage bubbling up inside him again.

"What did you just say to me?" he asked, articulating every word. But Alice said nothing. She merely extended her hand to him, holding out the envelope. Rory stared down at it but made no attempt to reach for it. When Rory didn't say anything more, Alice spoke.

"This is a packet of letters Mary wrote before she died," Alice explained. "She told me to give them to you when the time was right. I didn't know what she meant by that, but I suppose now is as good a time as any."

Rory reached out slowly to take the envelope from Alice. He held it with both hands, staring at the words written by Mary herself, maybe while she was resting in bed, or perhaps out on the deck while she enjoyed the warm breeze in her hammock. Either way, it didn't matter. Her fingers had spelled out the words "My Love" at some point in the recent past. Rory hadn't seen her handwriting in months. He looked up at Alice.

"Did you read them?" he demanded Alice.

"No," Alice replied, taken aback. If she was expecting any sort of response from Rory, it wasn't that. "I'm not that type of person, you know that, Rory."

Rory stared at the envelope and its seal, not wanting to break it. Mary's tongue had caressed the flap, and to rip it open would be to destroy a tiny bit that remained of his beloved. And what was inside…well, that very well might destroy him.

"Are you going to open it?" Dex asked finally.

"Would you," Rory asked him, his eyes red and swollen, "if it was Alice?"

"If it meant knowing I could hear from her one more time?" Dex replied. "Yes. No question about it."

"Well," Rory sighed, "I'm not likely to do it in front of you two then, am I?"

Alice and Dex looked at each other, then hesitantly made their way to the door. Just before they left Alice turned around.

"We'll leave the door open…you know, just in case," she said awkwardly. Rory stared at her with a look of disgust. When the two of them had finally left, Rory carefully broke the seal to the envelope. He poured the contents of it onto his bed, each letter in a different, smaller, white envelope. They were numbered 1-7. He found the envelope labeled 1 and tore it open, his excitement building. In it was a piece of paper, folded. He flattened it out and saw the sea of black cursive cascading it. He took a deep breath, his heart feeling like it was going to fly out of his chest. He looked down, and began to read:

Hello Darling,

Well. Here we are. Or you are, I guess. If you're reading this, either I beat this cancerous demon and left you for someone prettier, or felt so bad for its constant tormenting me that I decided to be the bigger person and give in to it. Either way, I expect you're missing me terribly. There is a lot I want to say that I couldn't in person. First of all, I am sorry. I am sorry that I couldn't wait to kick the bucket (assuming that's the route I went. If I am in Venice snogging Italians you can stop reading right now). I didn't want you to be a widower. Second of all, I know why you are reading this letter. You promised me you wouldn't cheat. But you did. You cheated. You cheated on the cancer. You wanted to go a different way, but that's not how this works. We stare down the barrel of the gun, remember? So you broke that promise to me. I'll forgive you this one time since, one, I don't really have a choice and, two, I've definitely broken promises now and again. Like my promise to "wait for you, so we go together." That was some rubbish.

What did I even hear that from, some disgustingly melancholy movie?

Anyway, I'm getting off track. You still have time, Rory. Time to live. I'm about to give you some tough love: You never let me live. You sheltered me and kept me safe and sound as long as possible. And I hated you for it. Would it have killed me to jump off of a moving train in the middle of nowhere, to dive out of an airplane, to climb a mountain? Probably not. It wouldn't have sped the process up any, either. So here's the deal. Read the rest of the letters I have thoughtfully written up for you. They are a list of things I want you to do, to experience for yourself. Show them to Alice and Dex. You're going to live the way you never let me. And you will do it because you love me. And I am making you do it because I love you. I want you to feel joy again, at least once, before you die. I know you will go soon after me. Even though you are stable at the moment, we both have noticed your body becoming weaker. So take these words and hang on to them for dear life: You will see me soon. Alice and Dex? What will they have once you're gone? I hate the fact that our best memories are the days we could go out to the supermarket for shopping or to a restaurant, just because we didn't feel too nauseated to do so. Please do not think for a second that I didn't need or want you with me every step of the way through this journey. I would have given up long ago if you hadn't waltzed into my life and saved me from myself. Please let me do the same for you. Finally, remember the verse I read to you every night last month. 1 Corinthians 15:54-55, When the perishable has been clothed with the imperishable, and the mortal with immortality, then the saying that is written will come true: "Death has been swallowed up in victory. Where, O death, is your victory? Where, O death, is your sting?"

Rest knowing that I am not dead, but resting well too. Do these things not for me, but for the Lord. And if by now you still do not share my sentiments about said Man of the Hour, trust me. This is all I ask.

With sincerest love (and apologies),

Your Mary.

P.S. Turn the page over for your first assignment.

When Rory was finished, he looked up from the page. He didn't know what he was expecting, but this certainly wasn't it. Mary had never precisely been overly expressive of her love, but she had never hurt him like this letter did. He had at least expected her to reiterate her love for him and encouraging words to keep him going. But to Rory, this was the antithesis of that. He turned the letter over, and there was the first thing she wanted him to do.

"Bloody hell," Rory breathed.

Rory got up from his bed and sauntered out to the kitchen, where Alice was chopping vegetables for supper. Dex was reading the paper at the kitchen table, and he looked up when Rory entered. He was still holding the letter and had a stunned look on his face.

Alice put the knife down and wiped her hands on her apron. "You finished it, then?" she asked. "Are you going to tell us what it said?"

"She's made me a list," he said quietly.

"What, like a to-do list?" asked Dex. He turned to Alice. "Is she still allowed to do that? Like, from beyond the grave?"

"What are you talking about, Rory?" Alice said, confused.

"She says she hated me for never letting her be adventurous," Rory replied. "To take risks. I thought having cancer was a pretty big risk, but apparently, it wasn't a big enough adrenaline rush for Mary's liking." His voice hitched.

"What exactly is it that she wants you to do?" asked Dex, confused.

Rory tossed him the sheet of paper. "Read number one for yourself," he murmured.

Alice walked up behind and read over Dex's shoulder:

"'Number one: Steal a pregnancy test from Wilko. Love! This will be hilarious! And if you get caught, tell them that you're late and think you might be pregnant. But also, don't get caught. Because if you do, you're going have to go back and do it again. I know this doesn't seem very fair (or adventurous), but never fear. These tasks I have laid out for you will become increasingly more exciting.'"

The couple looked at Rory.

"She wants you to steal a pregnancy test?" asked Dex, slightly amused.

"What kind of game is she playing, right?" said Rory incredulously.

"I think it's funny," said Alice, laughing.

"It's ridiculous," argued Dex. "I mean, obviously he's not going to do it." He gave Rory a furtive glance.

"Right," replied Rory. "Of course not." He took the letter from Dex and looked at Mary's words. How her cursive slanted so that the whole paragraph seemed to be going down a slope. "Except that I'm the man who never gave her any sort of excitement. Who took care of her and nursed her and held her when her fever was so high that she convulsed. She is rubbing it in my face. And she's not allowed to play games, not now. Dammit, Mary," and he tossed the piece of paper across the table. Alice retrieved it.

"I'll go with you!" she said brightly. Dex turned to her with the same look he gave Rory.

"What?!" he exclaimed.

"It'll be funny," Alice said, trying to convince him. "And frankly, Rory, you haven't left the flat since you got here. You need this. For Mary's sake."

Dex looked at her with admiration. "She's right, mate," said Dex. "You need help. Now, either we can admit you to a ward, and you get the drugs that will keep you in a haze for weeks, or you can get your high off an adrenaline rush. The choice is yours."

Four

"This is a mistake," Rory reiterated for the tenth time since he and Alice left the flat.

"No, it's not. It's funny," insisted Alice.

The two of them were on their way to the Wilko two blocks away from their flat. Rory had tried to turn back three times, but Alice dragged him out the door.

"Come on, we used to nick stuff all the time, what's got your knickers in a wad this time?" said Alice.

"Uh, the fact that we're supposedly adults now?" Rory replied.

"Or at least one of us is, I guess," he muttered.

"Yeah, I guess so," Alice said, smiling at him. "Oh, come on, Ror," she slipped her arm through his, picking up her pace. "Live a little."

When they approached the convenient store, Alice turned to Rory.

"Right," she said, putting up the hood of her jacket and pulling out her phone. "Ready?" "Whatever," Rory pushed on the door to the convenient store, and the pair entered.

"Wait, hold on," said Alice, fiddling with her mobile.

"What are you doing with that?" asked Rory warningly.

"Filming you!" Alice said. "I promised Dex."

"Ugh," said Rory, disgusted. He looked around the store.

There was a checkout girl at the front register, and two people in aisle two, looking at toothpaste.

"They'll be at the back," Alice said.

Rory couldn't help but notice a metal detector right before the exit. He shot Alice a worried look.

"Don't worry," she whispered reassuringly, eyeing the detector. "This place is rubbish, I bet it doesn't even work." They continued walking toward the back of the store.

"I still can't believe I'm doing this," Rory muttered. He wandered around, slightly aimlessly, until they reached aisle 6. He walked down toward the end of the corridor, Alice watching him from her phone. Once they reached the pregnancy tests, Rory stood there eyeing them.

"What's the problem?" whispered Alice.

Rory looked at her. "I don't know which one to take."

Alice snickered from behind her phone. "I don't think it matters, Ror."

Rory looked timidly at the variety of options. He had no idea there would be so many to choose from. What was the difference between one that could tell you three days before the other? Were couples really that impatient? He and Mary had, of course, discussed the idea of children, but neither saw it as a reality, given their unreliable health. Mary's body proved to be unable to hold a pregnancy successfully, and adoption was out of the question. Why take an orphan in when in a few years he would just be parentless again? That was Rory's thinking. They didn't bring up the subject of kids often, given what happened, for even though Rory knew Mary agreed with him, he couldn't help but notice she became sad, even distant, when they did.

Rory reached for the cheapest test he could find and smoothly put it in the pocket of is zipped up jumper. The bulge was fairly obvious, but he kept both his hands in his pockets to make it less conspicuous. "Let's go," Rory nodded to the front. He led the way, Alice still filming him from behind. Rory nodded and smiled to the teenage girl behind the counter the front, who smiled shyly back. The two partners in crime proceeded with confidence through the detectors. Rory reached to open the door, but that was when the alarm went off.

The shelf stacker who the two friends hadn't seen earlier emerged from behind an aisle to see what the noise was about.

"Oi!" he yelled to Rory and Alice, who turned around quickly, facing him. "What have you got there, mate?" The man, who had to have been about the same age as the two friends, yelled at Rory, who at this point looked obviously guilty. "Go on, empty your pockets."

Alice watched, still through her phone, as Rory pulled out the pregnancy test box. She cringed.

"You're stealing a pregnancy test?" the chap said, whose tone suggested that he couldn't tell if he was angry or amused.

"Why do you need one of those?"

Rory stared blankly at the young man for several seconds, sizing him up. Skinny and pimply, he didn't seem extremely athletic. And the test itself cost three pounds at most. Then, out of nowhere, he remembered for a split second what it was like to hear Mary laugh.

"I'm...late?" Rory offered.

"Run!" yelled Alice.

Rory didn't need to be told again. Nor did he need the accidentally forceful shove Alice gave him; he was already running. And laughing. For the first time in a month, he was laughing and couldn't stop himself. He laughed when he looked behind him and saw the shelf stacker trying to chase them. He laughed as the young checkout girl's mouth dropped open at the scene. And he laughed when he and Alice reached the flat, and Alice tripped going up the stairs. It was far from the smoothest crime, though it hadn't exactly been difficult to pull off.

When Rory and Alice reached the top of the stairs and made it inside, Rory's ribs hurt from laughing so hard. He was also out of breath, as he was not used to exerting that much energy at once, and was already feeling the consequences. For once, though, he didn't care.

"That's the stupidest thing I've ever done," Rory panted.

"That's the stupidest thing you've ever done? That's just sad, Ror," judged Alice.

"I'm going back tomorrow and paying for it," Rory panted.

"You are returning to the scene of the crime?" Alice laughed. "You truly are daft."

They limped to the kitchen. "I'm so out of shape," complained Alice to Dex, who was sitting at the kitchen table, writing up reports for his work.

"Not as out of shape as the chap trying to chase us for half a mile," replied Rory, and that sent the two of them into another fit of giggles.

"You two back from the playground already?" Dex asked, amused.

Alice wrapped her arms around his chest, the phone in one hand. "Oh, don't be jealous, you. I filmed it for you." She showed him the video.

"Oh, very nice," commented Dex. "Way to panic, Ror." When he didn't hear a snarky comeback, he looked up. Rory had left.

"Where'd you go, mate?"

Rory re-entered the kitchen with a somber look on his face and his hands behind his back.

"I have something to tell you guys," Rory said seriously.

Alice stood up, concerned. "What is it?"

Rory held up the pregnancy test that he had taken out of the box.

"I'm not pregnant!" he announced.

Dex laughed, and Alice let out an exasperated sigh. "Rory! You can't do that to us."

"You sure you waited long enough to tell, mate?" was Dex's response. "Those things are time-sensitive, you know."

"Here, see for yourself." Rory held the stick out to Dex.

"Get that thing away from me!" Dex knocked the test out of Rory's hand, sending it flying toward Alice. She leaped out of the way, screaming.

"That's alright," said Rory, smiling. "There's more where that came from." He held up another one and tossed it at Dex. Dex stood up clumsily, knocking over his chair.

"Rory, you bastard!" yelled Dex, but he was laughing. He ran after Rory, who was already headed for his bedroom. In the kitchen Alice could hear her two best friends yelling and roughhousing, reminding her of the good times they used to have together. She looked at her phone and thought to herself, Oh, Mary. If only you could see your Rory now.

The laughter that filled the flat was short-lived, as Dex had scheduled an appointment for Rory with his new oncologist for that Friday. Rory was less than excited about this excursion. Apart from the shoplifting he had committed the other day, Rory had not left the flat since moving in with Alice and Dex. He didn't even know this new doctor; it was someone Dex had a connection with at the hospital.

Apparently, he wasn't accepting new patients, but he had

taken on

Rory's case as a favour for Dex. Dr. Sylvester, his oncologist back in

York, had been his doctor ever since he was diagnosed. Even when he moved, he kept in touch with his doctor and phoned him when he had emergency questions. Rory could already tell, after waiting in the strange doctor's office for ninety minutes with no sign of him, that he preferred Dr. Sylvester.

"Where the hell is Dr. Epstein?" Alice voiced what Rory was thinking as he sat next to her. Dex was pacing back and forth and had been doing so since they got there. "He's got us waiting here an hour and a half and doesn't even care that we're freaking the hell out. I mean, why would the nurses tell us we need to talk to him straight away if Rory's blood work had come back alright?"

"Physicians are busy, Alice," Dex replied through biting his fingernails. He had stopped pacing and was now staring out the picture window. There was an overcast outside, as there often was in London at this time of year.

"Yes, yes, you would know, wouldn't you?" At times, Alice got a bit annoyed with Dex when he played the whole 'I'm a doctor, I know what I'm talking about' card. It was all good and fine when she had a question about an illness she was certain she had, and he was quick to assure her she didn't have malaria, as she had never traveled to Africa.

"I wasn't trying to be—-" Dex began, but just then Dr.

Epstein swung open the office door. "Never mind," Dex muttered. But neither Alice nor Rory heard him. They had both stood up, and Rory stuck out his hand to shake Dr. Epstein's. However, the oncologist was busy reviewing Rory's chart, which he had picked up only a couple of seconds before entering,

49

and was too engrossed in it to notice. Rory and Alice sat down, exchanging an uncomfortable glance as Dr. Epstein took a seat behind his desk. Dex tore himself away from the window and stood behind Alice and Rory.

"Well," Dr. Epstein began, "let's get down to business. No use beating around the bush. Rory, according to your PET scan, the tumor that began in your femur has metastasized to your lungs. That would explain the dyspnea you've been experiencing. Now, it says here in your chart that you were under astute observation for this in Wales. I'm afraid that negligence to keep up with your prescribed chemotherapy and missing your radiation appointments has had a detrimental, although to be quite frank, expected, consequence."

Rory's head felt like someone had waterboarded him over and over again. He couldn't wrap his brain around the words coming from this strange man. "My wife just died," was all he could manage.

"I'm sorry for your loss," Dr. Epstein replied curtly. Though in Rory's opinion, this man didn't seem to understand the concept of sympathy. "I see that you had a bone graft taken from your right hip to your left distal femur back in 2004. And that along with the chemotherapy was enough to prevent metastasis. The work your body has been put through these last ten years has prolonged the ultimate effect of the cancer, but I'm afraid any attempt to prolong it would be in vain, given your recent history of noncompliance. However, if you're ready to continue your treatment, survival rate of osteosarcoma once it has reached the lungs is 50 percent."

The three of them took a moment to process what the doctor had so bluntly just told them. Dex was the first to pluck up the nerve to speak. "So, wait, what does that mean?"

"Dr. Gallagher, you are an intelligent man," Dr. Epstein responded, looking up for the first time since sitting down. "You are well aware of the effect your brother's cancer will have on him when it stops responding to treatment."

"Doctor, please," pleaded Alice, her eyes wide and shining. Dr. Epstein sighed. He looked at Rory, for the first time, in the eye. Rory stared back at him.

"We will continue to prescribe your current medications, in hopes of the best possible outcome. The trouble in breathing you reported is only going to worsen as time goes on, and the pain you've been feeling in your bones is going to increase. There are, of course, medications we can prescribe to make you more comfortable, and you can receive outpatient treatment here three times a week. However, unless your body spontaneously decides to respond to treatment, you're looking at about a month. Maybe two."

"Two months?" Dex straightened up. "To live?"

"If we're being optimistic, then yes," Dr. Epstein replied bluntly.

"Two months," repeated Dex, who was slightly in shock.

Dr. Epstein was still looking at Rory. "I am sorry, Rory. I know you have battled with this for years. Osteosarcomas usually have a high survival rate, if they don't metastasize to the lung. You're just one of the unlucky ones. " He turned to Dex. "If you will excuse me, I have other patients who are waiting for me. I will leave you three here to digest this information and discuss it among yourselves. If you have any questions, there is a number you can call, on this card here." He pulled out a card with his office number on it. Rory reached out and accepted it from him silently. Dr. Epstein gathered the manila folders on his desk and stacked them together, leaving the three of them in silence as he exited the office.

The ride home on the tube was about as cheerful as the visit to the hospital had been. The train was hot and crowded, and Rory was beginning to feel nauseated. Alice gave up her seat a little way into the trip so he could sit down. Both Dex and Alice had to hold the rail for support as the car lurched forward at every stop. None of them had mentioned what they heard in the office. Alice had begun to try and discuss the matter, but Rory couldn't take it, not there. He got up swiftly, feeling like he was going to be sick, and stormed out of the building, Dex and Alice trailing behind him.

"Dr. Epstein is a complete arse," Alice finally blurted out as the car lurched forward again. "Is there any way we can get a second opinion?"

"Alice, the physician being an arse doesn't change the facts," Dex chastised her.

"But two months! He delivered Rory's death sentence with nothing more than a glance and a nod! How can you be okay with this?

You work there, for goodness' sake."

"Dr. Epstein is not my biggest problem at the moment, Alice," Dex said, frustrated at her. He turned his attention to his brother. "You haven't said a word. Not one. What's going through your head, little brother?"

Rory shook his head. "I dunno. This is the moment we've been preparing for for nearly ten years now, though, isn't it? And now that it's here I just...I don't know what to make of it."

Alice bent down to Rory's level and put a comforting hand on his shoulder.

"How are you going to tell Mum and Dad?" Dex wanted to

know.

Alice looked back up at him with disdain.

"Dex!"

"Come on, Ror," Dex continued, "You can't think that you're going to get away with not speaking to Mum and Dad until the day you die. I won't allow it."

"They would much rather hear from you that I've died than from me at all," Rory contested.

"That's not true, and you know it," Dex snarled. "You're being stubborn, and it won't get you anywhere now."

"They're your parents, Ror," Alice appealed. "I don't know what that means to you now, but—-"

"I'll tell you what it means," interrupted Rory. "It means that I wrote to them and tried to make amends with them for years to no avail. It is completely up to them to communicate with me, something I have been trying to do for years. I'm not going to try and start now just because…because it's real."

"What is?" asked Dex.

"My inevitable demise," said Rory bitterly.

"Put it like that, and you sound like the victim of a murderous lunatic," commented Alice sarcastically. "Don't let yourself believe your life is that interesting."

Rory looked at her. Before he could help it, a chuckle bubbled up and escaped him. "I'm not trying to get in touch with Mum or Dad," he restated. "Please, Dex. Don't make me do this. It won't turn out well, and you know it."

Dex didn't say anything for a while. Finally, the train came to a halt, and the three of them got off. As they trotted up the steps from the station, emerging into the sunlight, Dex conceded.

"Alright," he said. "Alright. You won't have to do anything on your own. I'll admit it's not fair to you."

"Thank you," Rory sighed with relief.

"We'll tell them together," Dex continued. "Alice and I will do it with you."

Rory snorted. "And how exactly do you plan to do that?"

Dex looked hesitant. "I have…something of an idea."

The sound of the buzzer indicating company woke Rory with a start. He had fallen asleep as soon as he had gotten home, thanks to the magic of a sleeping pill Dex had given him. Before plunging into his deep slumber, Dex had told him not to worry, that Alice and he were going to take care of everything. Rory realized now he should have been warier of what his brother's plan actually was. From the sound of the buzzer, he had an inkling of what was about to occur.

Dex was the one who answered the door. Alice was busy bustling in the kitchen and had been there since that afternoon. After Dex had given Rory a sleeping aid, he phoned his parents, inviting them over for one of Alice's home-cooked meals. The problem is, Alice could cook about as well as Rory could cure himself of cancer. But she had always been able to improvise with (quite a bit) of help from Dex when the Gallaghers came over.

"Dad!" Dex's relationship with his father was possibly the antithesis of that which Rory had with the man. Arthur had always been so proud of Dex, who had managed to get accepted into his top choice of university, and later get into the medical program based on excellent marks and recommendations. In other words, Arthur had never felt guilty about Dex's outcome because of his lack of financial stability. Rory, on the other hand, had missed so much school due to his illness that he eventually had to be educated from home by his mother, leaving his father to work extra hours at their family-owned sports shop just to pay off their house in York.

"Dex, my boy!" The proud man puffed out his chest as he embraced his son in a firm hug. A small figure with blonde hair poked her head around Arthur.

"Oh, dear, it's so good to see you!" Sarah hugged her son as well.

"Mum, thanks for coming," Dex returned the hug.

"We were just so pleased to get a call from you! What a nice surprise it was, we had no plans tonight at all. The Wilmots canceled us, and we thought we were going to have to stay in like old married folk!"

"We are old married folk," Arthur smiled as he took his wife's coat and hung it on the rack in the living room.

"Well, come on into the kitchen. Alice has been slaving away in there for hours on something that smells delicious." Dex ushered his parents toward the kitchen.

"I wouldn't say hours." Alice came out from the kitchen, taking off her oven mitts and untying her apron. "Or delicious. But hopefully satisfying! Or at least competent..." she smiled nervously.

"Oh, sweetheart, come here," Sarah gestured toward Alice. "It's so lovely to see you."

"It's good to see you too, Sarah," Alice replied, hugging her. Sarah had always been like a second mother to Alice, ever since she had been in primary school with Rory. Alice always felt comfortable going over to the Gallaghers' house; it was small and quiet, but she liked it that way. It was different from the three-story house her parents owned just a few streets away, and that was a comfort for her. She usually never even knocked on their door, always feeling welcome enough to let herself in, even up to Rory's room without indication.

However, once she began to date Dex, she began to knock before going inside.

"Well, everyone come along before the food gets cold," Alice said in a high-pitched voice. She was nervous, and Dex knew it wasn't just because of the food.

The three of them followed Alice to the table, which she had set perfectly. They had used nice dishes and cutlery, and the roast Alice had made looked delectable. But something else registered with Arthur as soon as he saw the table.

"There are five places set, is someone else joining us?"

Before either Dex or Alice could answer, Rory appeared in the doorway behind his parents.

"Hullo, Dad." His voice was deep and monotonous, yet it resonated in the silence for what seemed like hours. Arthur and Sarah whipped their heads around. When they saw their son, Arthur's eyes turned dark, his face and neck grew red. Sarah's eyes, on the contrary, lit up.

"I assume Dex didn't relay the message that I was joining you," Rory continued. "Or that I was even living here."

At first, the two of them just stared at their son. Neither of them spoke until Sarah finally broke the silence.

"Oh, Rory," she breathed. "We were going to phone. We heard about Mary. We are so, so sorry. We just wanted to make sure you had enough time to grieve before upsetting you by getting in touch." The guilt in her voice lingered in the air even after she had stopped talking.

"God forbid you pick up the phone for a quick chat, right?" Rory said bitterly. This was enough to set Arthur off.

"Don't speak to your mother like that, boy!"

"Alright, alright, everyone just calm down." Alice was a

nervous wreck when it came to tense situations. Ever since her parents' separation, she couldn't stand them and would do anything to avoid them. "I lied earlier. It actually has taken me hours to make this supper, so just sit down, the lot of you, and enjoy it before it gets too cold."

Alice was sure even Dex wouldn't be allowed to speak to the Gallaghers like this, but she was always an exception in their household.

Despite Alice's rude tone, everyone followed her orders and took seats at the table. Alice took the head seat, Dex sitting next to her. Rory followed Dex and found himself sitting across from his father. Sarah joined the table on the other side of Alice, rubbing her back.

"It's good to see you're doing well, Rory," his mother commented.

"I look well, do I?" Rory said, his eyes drooping, his hair a mess from neglecting to comb it after many sleepless nights.

"You respect your mother, now, boy," Arthur reprimanded Rory.

"Alice, this supper is amazing," Dex said, trying to prolong the inevitable conversation that would accompany the meal.

"Thanks, love, it's your mother's recipe," Alice said anxiously. "Sarah? How did I do?"

"Oh, dear, it's wonderful," Sarah replied, avoiding looking at both her husband and youngest son. "Well done, you."

"Don't think you're off the hook," Arthur said, this time speaking to Dex.

"What for?" Dex asked incredulously.

"You know bloody well what for!" Arthur had tossed down his fork onto the plate, causing a clank. "For luring us here under false pretenses! Trying to trick us in to being in the same room as your brother!"

"Oh, Arthur," Sarah said, attempting to be the voice of reason, "I hardly think that's what their intentions are here."

"For hiding him here—-" continued Arthur, not listening to his wife.

"Sorry?" cried Dex indignantly. "I'm not hiding anyone here. I told you I was going to help him find a place to stay."

"You know he's only trying to freeload off of you!" retorted Arthur. "Now that he doesn't have the security of his posh girlfriend or her parents—-"

"Arthur!" Sarah finally addressed her husband's outburst. Arthur turned to face her.

"You know you're thinking the exact same as me!" he accused his wife.

"I'm dying!" Rory couldn't take it anymore. All of the nonsense his parents were giving his brother. The fact that none of them were talking directly to him. He knew the reason Dex had orchestrated supper. He figured if he could shock everyone, they would shut up. It worked.

"What did you just say?" Sarah asked breathlessly, breaking the silence that had fallen over the supper table. Rory was always the quieter of her two boys, still trailing a little too far behind his brother. Never speaking up, and certainly never shouting.

"I went to the doctor today," Rory continued, refusing to look anywhere but his plate. "They conducted a blood test and some scans. My bone cancer has caught up to my lungs and…and according to my doctor, my prognosis isn't looking that great."

"But what does that mean?" Sarah's voice was shaking. Rory didn't answer her at first. Finally, he looked up into her watering blue eyes.

"I've been given about two months," he declared.

Sarah drew in a sharp breath. "Two months?"

Rory went back to averting her look. "Yeah."

"TWO MONTHS!?" Sarah stood up, the sound of her chair moving back making a screeching sound against the hardwood floor, similar to that of nails on a blackboard.

"What should it matter to you two?" Rory's voice was still level, but he felt rage bubbling up in his stomach. "As far as Dad's concerned, I died the day I moved away with Mary. I was erased from your lives. And you," he pointed to Sarah, "if you really cared about my prognosis, you wouldn't have let him," he pointed to Arthur, "control you like a puppet, keeping you from seeing or talking to me!"

"That's enough!" Arthur stood up too, throwing his napkin on his plate.

"Is this what this supper was about?" Sarah's voice broke. "You invited us here so you could tell us your…your death sentence?"

"Mum, don't you see?" Rory's voice began to crack as well.

"This isn't news to you. I've been dying since I was fifteen years old.

You're just now realizing the reality of my mortality, and now it's too

late."

Sarah looked as though her son had taken the knife he had used to cut his roast and thrust it into her chest. She opened her mouth, perhaps to plead with her son, but Arthur spoke first.

"Come along, Sarah. We're leaving."

"Dad, please, he's your son!" Dex implored.

Arthur looked at Dex. "I have one son. One son who did not walk out on this family, who did not cause his mother more pain than she was capable of bearing, and one son who has proven himself a man. Anyone else is no son of mine."

Arthur turned swiftly and walked out of the kitchen with a long stride. Everyone jumped slightly as the door to the flat slammed behind him. Sara was sitting still as a statue, looking at Rory.

Rory looked up at her from across the table.

"Mum…Mummy, please. Please don't let it end like this." Tears had welled up in Rory's eyes as he begged his mother.

Sarah looked back at him, tears in her own eyes. She quietly stood up, pushed her chair in, and scuttled out of the kitchen. The door opened and closed gently behind her.

Rory covered his face with his hands, his shoulders heaving up and down. His hands were not sufficient to stifle the sound of his sobbing. Dex put an arm almost absentmindedly around him, staring blankly at the two chairs his parents had just abandoned. Alice simply gazed at the two, and while they sat there, she began to clear the table.

Five

Rory went to his room that night without a word. Alice and Dex assumed he had gone to bed, but in fact he dug out the envelope with all of Mary's letters. He fished around until he found the smaller white one labeled 2. This one was much shorter than her previous one, and it did not take him long to figure out her intention in writing it.

Hello Love,

If you're reading this letter, I hope it means that you've done what I asked in the previous one. To which I must say, bravo! I knew you had it in you. Don't fear, I'm not asking anything of the sort this time. Instead, I just ask that you remember. Close your eyes, and take time to remember the first time we met. Sometimes we forget where we've come from because we're so caught up in where we are now. But I remember the very first time we spoke, and I hope you remember it too.

You definitely weren't into my strangeness. We don't even have to pretend you found me slightly charming. You thought I was absolutely mental. That's alright, though. Those love at first sightings are a bit overrated. I didn't fall in love with your personality the first time I met you. But you were new, and you were interesting. And you let me just talk and talk. I loved that. There was also a subtle sadness about you that was beautiful. Is it any wonder that it only took until that next week before we were both ditching Support Group to snog in the alley? We could not have been more different from each other. So naturally, we were perfect together. Remember 1 Corinthians 13:13? "And now these three remain: faith, hope, and love.

But the greatest of these is love."

Your Mary

Winter, 2004

Rory reluctantly opened the door to the community center and let it swing shut behind him. He looked around at all the kids there, some of them older, some of them, in Rory's opinion, who were too young to even know what specific medical terms meant. But here they all were. Everyone was mingling, gathered around the table with tea and store bought biscuits, neither of which seemed appealing to him at the moment. Since starting chemotherapy a month ago, Rory barely had an appetite for anything, and only ate when he was coaxed to do so by his mother. He found a chair against the wall and took a seat, slumping down in it. He crossed his arms and continued to scan the room, judging the mundanity of it all.

He didn't see her at first. She came up from his left side, and he was staring off to the right at a kid who had just been wheeled in by his mother. He didn't even know she was there until she spoke.

"Hodgkin's lymphoma," the girl said, sticking out her hand.

Rory's head whipped around and he found himself looking into the most unique eyes he had ever seen. His whole family, except for his mother, all had brown eyes. But this girl, she had what seemed like all the colors. Green, blue, and amber, even a hint of gold, all swirled together like a galaxy. It caught him off guard and he realized he had forgotten what she had said to him.

"Come again?" he asked blankly.

The girl repeated herself, her arm still extended. "Hodgkin's lymphoma. It's my diagnosis. I assume you're here for Support Group, yes?"

Rory was still confused as to why this girl, whom he incidentally found extremely attractive, was talking to him.

"Come again?" he repeated.

"Group therapy." She finally lowered her hand, realizing he was not going to shake it. "Or are you looking for the theatre class? It meets next door."

"I'm…not an actor," Rory replied.

"Well, none of them are, really," the girl smiled. "It's the local community theater."

"Right," Rory said. As attractive as this girl was, she wasn't going to intervene with his plan not to make friends or participate. But his disinterested tone seemed to have no effect on her.

"So you are here for Group then," she said, leaning against the wall next to him.

"Uh, yeah, I suppose," Rory said.

"So what are you then?" she asked.

"Uh, I have osteosarcoma in my left leg," he replied.

"Nice," the girl nodded. "We have an assortment here. Some of these kids aren't even dying from cancer, they've got some other life sucking disease. Some aren't even sick at all, but their siblings or friends are. We don't have a bone cancer yet, funnily enough. You're

our first!"

"Well, glad I could do you all a favour, I suppose," Rory said. This girl was strange, acting nonchalantly about all the diseases that plagued the room.

"Why don't you come and sit in the circle," the girl offered cheekily. "I don't think we're all going to fit against the wall. You seem to have taken the only available spot."

"Oh, that's fine," Rory said quickly. "I'm just going to stay here, thanks. I'm not going to be here very long, anyway."

"Well, that's a bit narcissistic, isn't it?" the girl said, her eyebrows raised.

"Sorry?" Rory asked, alarmed.

"I mean, none of us are exactly going to be here very long," the girl continued. "Except Nicholas over there who only comes because his sister who is ill refuses to do so."

"No," said Rory, "I just meant I had to come in here to make it look like I was staying. Once this thing starts, I'm ditching."

"Oh, I understand," the girl said knowingly. "Your parents forced you to come to this."

"Yeah," Rory told her.

"That's a common thing around here," she said. "I promise it helps though. At least to talk about it. Obviously, it's not going to help physiologically. Although, you know, I've been reading about a study some genius scientist somewhere conducted attempting to prove a correlation between positive thinking and the lifespan of people with a terminal illness. It was fascinating."

"Right," was all Rory could think to say. This girl sure was a talker, he thought.

"So what's your name then? I'm Mary." "Uh, I don't think so," Rory shook his head. "I'm sorry, I don't understand," Mary said.

"I already told you, I'm bailing," Rory replied, standing up. "So it was really nice to meet you, er, Mary, but I've got better ways to spend my time."

As Rory turned to leave, the instructor made an announcement from the center of the room.

"Right then, everyone," the she called, "it's about time to circle up. I see we have a new face with us today! Mary, do you want to introduce your friend?"

Mary whispered out of the corner of her mouth to Rory, "It's too late now. Better tell me your name or you're on your own."

Rory turned halfway around from the door through which he was so close to escaping. "It's Rory," he whispered back.

"This is Rory," Mary announced to the room. "He's got cancer in his leg."

"We're so glad to have you join us, Rory," the instructor replied. "I'm Martha. Please, have a seat in the circle." She gestured to the chairs in the center of the room. Rory eyed them with a look of disgust mixed with dread. Mary placed her hand in the crook of his elbow and guided him to the circle. The two of them sat down next to each other, and Rory looked around at the other members, up close this time. He was sickened by the whole thing, knowing that he was one of them now. He slumped down as far as he could in his chair, his legs extended so far that his Chuck Taylors reached the middle of the circle.

"Alright," the instructor said. "Let's begin with introductions." Rory rolled his eyes and slumped even further down in his chair. His eyes darted to each unfortunate adolescent as they went around the room, saying their name and diagnosis, as if one could not exist without the other. After Mary's turn, everyone looked at Rory expectantly.

"I'm Rory, like she said," Rory said, monotone.

"We usually ask first-timers to tell us a bit of their story,"
Martha said, obviously trying to prod more information out
of him. "My story?" Rory asked, eyebrows so far up on his
forehead they nearly reached his widow's peak.

"Yeah, sort of like a snapshot of your journey through your
ailment. When did you find out about your diagnosis, and how
are you dealing with your circumstances?"

That was a bit of a loaded question, Rory thought. He hadn't
even really discussed how he felt about his cancer with his
family, and definitely felt no desire to do so with this lot. Out
of the corner of his eye, he felt Mary's eyes on him. He couldn't
figure out why this made his palms start to sweat. He quickly
panicked at the thought of possibly having to hold hands and
sing or pray together, and he didn't want the girl to think he
was repulsive for having clammy hands. He attempted to rub
the perspiration off onto his jeans as casually as possible and
hoped it looked like he was preparing to expose his life story to
the group of strangers.

"Er," he began. Great, he thought. What a brilliant way to
start. This girl definitely thinks you're an idiot. He stopped this
train of thought before it derailed. Why did he care what the
chatty girl thought? Rory cleared his throat.

"A couple of months ago, my leg was hurting me a lot. Not just
aches and pains, but at times it hurt to bear weight on it at all. It
even swelled to twice its size. I'd come home from school and
just lie down in bed. I didn't feel like doing any work outside
with my dad or playing a game of football with my brother and
his friends. That's when my mum noticed something was up.
So she took me to some doctor at

York Hospital. A bone scan revealed a tumor in my leg, and
I've already begun chemotherapy and radiation. If that doesn't

help, they're going to take a chunk of bone out of my hip and replace the part of my leg that has the tumor with the hip bone. They call it 'salvage surgery,' or something like that I think. Which sounds more hardcore than painful. But I'm kind of hoping that doesn't have to happen."

When Rory finished, he looked around the circle at all the blank stares. He had divulged much more than he had intended to, and suddenly felt self-conscious that maybe not everyone shared every detail of their diagnosis their first time at Group.

"Thank you, Rory, for sharing," Martha said gently. "We will be keeping you in thought and prayer."

Out of the corner of his eyes, he glanced at Mary. He saw her body turned toward him, eyes wide and sympathetic. Why should you feel bad for me? Rory wondered. Why should any of us feel sorry for each other? We're all going through our own personal hells. Surely the human heart isn't capable of enough empathy to go around the entire circle. Then again, he thought, maybe it's just my heart that's not capable of that.

The meeting lasted a total of sixty-two minutes. Rory knew this because every four or five minutes, he would glance down at his watch, expecting for the minute hand to have covered much more circumference than it had. During that time, people cried, giggled, sniffed, offered tissues, offered advice, and one person even got so angry at his own bad luck that he cursed God. When this happened, Rory heard Mary take a sharp intake of breath. She didn't say anything, though.

Rory was the first to leave when the session was over. He snuck out while the rest of the group had their eyes closed, praying. He didn't bother to be inconspicuous, either, letting the door slam shut behind him. He stood at the curb outside the community center, waiting for his mother to come to pick him up.

"Rory!" the familiar female voice called from behind him. "Rory, wait!"

He turned around. He wasn't interested in talking to Mary now, and he looked harder for his mother. Maybe if he saw her coming, he could start walking and meet her before she got to the building. He didn't want to expand on his story, and he was afraid that if he heard any more of hers (or anyone else's for that matter), his heart might not be able to handle it, and would actually break. But he didn't see his mother's car, and the girl caught up to him.

"So what did you think of your first group session?" Mary wanted to know.

"Daft," Rory replied. "Just like I knew it would be."

Mary looked in the same direction Rory was staring off into. "Waiting for your mum to pick you up, then? Me as well. I could walk, but my parents don't like me overdoing it. I don't even live that far away, just a couple of miles. Still, Mum and Dad don't really approve of me doing anything active. Just in case, you know?"

Rory didn't know why this girl continued to try to make conversation with him. Sure, she was attractive, but frankly, he found how perky she was to be a bit of a nuisance. But it was nice talking to another girl that wasn't Alice for once. "Just in case of what?"

"That's what I'm saying!" said Mary, smiling. "I don't know! I mean, what could possibly happen to me that's worse than what already has? I mean, getting hit by a double decker would yield more instantaneous results I suppose, but—-"

"Are you always this talkative?" Rory interrupted.

Mary thought for a minute. "Not really," she admitted. "I

usually don't have anyone to chat with. Not since my parents began homeschooling me. So what about your parents?"

"I'm not homeschooled."

"No, I mean are they overprotective of you, too?" "I suppose."

"What do you do when you're not in therapy?" Mary wanted to know.

"I don't know," said Rory. "I help out in the shop. My parents own Trainers for Life on the corner of Gillygate and Lord Mayors Walk. What about you?" He turned his body toward her for the first time since meeting her, finally giving her his full attention.

"I like to read," said Mary. "My parents own the bookshop on Patrick Pool."

"What do you like to read?"

"Books," Mary smiled.

Rory laughed. "What kind of books?"

Mary shrugged. "All kinds! Mostly about travel. I can't actually go anywhere, but with books, I can at least pretend. I can go away for hours, days, and no one even misses me. I can visit New York City, the Isle of Skye, even Australia! And I never have to leave the comfort of my bed."

"Comfort, or confinement?" Rory said pointedly.

Mary stared down at her laced-up Oxfords. "My parents mean well, they really do. It's just…travel is expensive. And shop owners only make so much, as I'm sure you're aware."

At that moment, Rory's mother pulled up in her car.

"Well, that's my mum," Rory said, but he wasn't as relieved to see her as he thought he would be. "It's been quite…interesting meeting you, Mary."

"Aren't you glad you didn't bail?" she asked.

"Er…we'll see next week," Rory said hesitantly.

"I'll be here," Mary said smiling.

Rory got in the passenger side of his mother's car. As they drove away, Rory glanced back at Mary, who was waving to him from the sidewalk.

"Well?" Sarah pulled Rory's attention back to her. "Was it as traumatizing as you anticipated?"

"It was alright," Rory said, smiling slightly.

"Did you make a friend?" his mother wanted to know. "I saw you standing with that girl."

"Mum, don't," Rory said, erasing the smile from his face as quickly as it appeared.

"Alright, I'm sorry!" his mother conceded. "It's just you're not very social as it is, Ror. Sometimes it seems like your only friend is Alice. Maybe you and that girl will be able to see more of each other."

"Yeah, maybe," Rory tried to get his hopefulness from his mother.

"Don't look so glum, Rory," his mother said. "This could be good for you. Who knows, that girl may be just the pick-me-up you've been needing."

Rory didn't say anything. Instead, he turned away and stared out the window for the remainder of the car ride.

Six

Dex wrapped his robe around him a little tighter as he stepped out onto the front steps of his flat. The sun had just come up, and it was freezing. His flannel pajamas were not sufficient in trapping in his body heat, and his robe provided very little insulation. He inhaled the smoke from the cigarette he was smoking and tried to focus on how cold he was, rather than the memories of the night before. He heard the door open behind him and turned his head, hoping it wasn't Rory. He wasn't ready to face him or the situation yet. Not before he had his morning coffee.

Alice pulled a red jumper over her head and sat down next to Dex on the top step.

"I didn't think you still smoked," she said disapprovingly.

"I don't," said Dex. "I nicked one of these from Rory."

"Doesn't he know those things will kill him?" Alice wasn't a fan of smoking and couldn't stand the stench of it.

"I don't think his greatest concern is contracting lung cancer right at this moment," Dex said. Alice hung her head down, smiling.

"Right," she said. She lifted her head up to look at Dex. "Dex, we should talk about last night at supper with your family."

Dex snorted. "What family?" He inhaled from his cigarette,

then blew out. "And anyway, there's nothing to talk about. Everything Rory ever said, and I reprimanded him for saying, turned out to be true."

"What are you talking about?" asked Alice.

Dex sighed. "Our father is prideful. He's arrogant and neglectful. And he convinced our mother that Rory isn't the same son he was before he left all those years ago."

Alice finally asked the question that had been on her mind. "Why did Rory leave, anyway? I mean, I know how much he loved Mary. It just seemed like all of a sudden he had moved away and your parents never addressed it. They never went with us to visit."

Dex took a deep breath. "Dad worked hard, harder than he ever had in his entire life, to ensure that Rory and I both had the best lives we could. But it was never enough. We were always in debt. Mary's family was always offering to help us out financially, but Dad never accepted. And so when the opportunity in Wales came about...Well, you know the rest. And the Abels paid for everything; the move, their home, they covered it all. And if you ask me, Mary did more good for Rory than any of his meds ever did. The move made Mum and Dad so...infuriated. Hurt. They never spoke to him, never visited him. His only visitors were ever you and me."

Alice sat next to Dex in silence for a moment, letting this all sink in. "I...I never realized the magnitude of the dispute between them."

Dex took another breath of his cigarette. "Yeah, well, now last night makes sense to you. Mind you, I'm never speaking to that man again."

Alice tilted her head. "Of course you will, Dex, he's your dad."

Dex turned to her. "And Rory is his son. Blood relation means nothing in our family, Alice." He sat there for a while, staring at the people on their street getting in their cars, preparing to go to work. These people who didn't have a sick relative to worry about or parents who disowned their children. He rubbed his temple with his thumb and forefinger.

"God, what am I going to do?" he groaned.

Alice took the cigarette from Dex's hand and placed it on the step beneath her foot. She stepped on it, putting it out. She put an arm around her partner and began to rub his back.

"You carry on," she said, as if it was obvious. "For Rory. You be there for him, the way no other man in his life will. We make sure that his last months here are as happy and as comfortable as possible." Dex looked up at the love of his life. He knew that, as important as Rory was to him, he was just as important to Alice. Finally, he nodded.

Rory let days pass without reading a new letter from Mary. He wanted to make them last as long as possible. So he would read the first two over and over again. Finally, a week after the supper incident with his parents, he felt as though he deserved to open a new one. He took the envelope of letters out of the drawer in his nightstand and opened the one labeled 3.

Hello Darling,

Trains were always so fascinating to me. I guess I should specify that the conductors were always fascinating to me. At least, their lives were. Imagine getting to travel to a new place every day! That's the kind of life I wish I could have lived. I know pilots get to do that as well, but it's not the same. All they see is blue sky. Train conductors get to see the world, practically! They get to travel the lands, see animals, trees, and buildings. And that is beautiful to me.

I remember how long it took me to get you to see the beauty of this, too.

I'm not reminding you of all of this because I want you to give up everything and become a bum just to see the world, Rory, so relax. I'm saying I want you to take a risk. Be daring. Jump off the edge of the world and dare yourself to find your way back. Because you are lost right now, Ror. As I write this, I can see it already. You lost yourself in taking care of me, and it's time that you find the part of you that is just you again.

Jesus took his friends the disciples on adventures; it's how they bonded. He took them out to sea, to villages they had never been before and had parties with them. You, Alice, and Dex need to bond again. It's been years since it was just the three of you. Don't let that be such a bad thing.

With much love and admiration,
Your Mary

Spring, 2006

Mary had told Rory they were going to her favorite place. He assumed it would be a hole-in-the-wall tea room or an art museum, but instead she had dragged him to an open field. Rory wasn't sure what she found so exciting about it. "Wait for it," she had told him. Finally, they heard the horn of an oncoming train. She sprawled out on the grass and watched as the train sped past where they were sitting. Rory still wasn't sure what he was supposed to be waiting for. He didn't even know about Mary's obsession with trains until now. But he humoured her and watched it as intently as she did as it passed them by.

"My dad used to sing me a song about train jumpers," Mary said, her eyes still fixed on the train. "Hobos, he called them.

You wouldn't see them in the city, he would tell me. They ride on trains and travel from place to place, invisible to the rest of the world."

Rory just stared at her. "That's incredibly depressing," he said.

Mary shrugged. "I liked it. His father was a bobby. He would always tell my dad stories of having to chase these men from the trains.

They like to get their free rides in. Still, he would take pity on them.

Nowhere else to go, I suppose. Can you imagine, though, Rory?" She turned to him. "Being able to hop on a train one day and just go? Not having a care in the world, not knowing what you're going to eat for supper, what plans to work around your next doctor's appointment? What medicine you need to take at exactly which moment?"

Rory chuckled at her. "Are you saying you want to become a hobo?"

"I'm saying that I wish I had the privilege of being as carefree as that," said Mary. "Sometimes…sometimes I wish I didn't know I had cancer."

"That's stupid, Mary," Rory told her.

"No, it's not!" she argued. "Think about it. We're both inevitably going to die someday. These drugs that make us feel weak are just dragging it out. If I never found out I was ill, my parents probably would have let me travel, see the world! Jump off a bloody train, just for the hell of it."

"You want to jump off a moving train?" Rory said doubtfully.

Mary turned to look at him. "I want to live spontaneously. But that's not exactly a possibility with my condition and my parents."

Rory looked at her as she turned her attention back to the

train still going by.

"Martha from Group asked me what I wanted to be when I grew up," she told him. "I laughed at her and rolled my eyes. But she told me to seriously consider what I would like to be doing, ten years from now. It's taken me forever to think up an answer because I honestly never considered it before."

"Oh yeah?" Rory said. "What did you come up with?"

"I want to be a writer," Mary said confidently. "I want to travel. I want to travel, and write about what I see, what I learn, what I experience. I want to write a book just like my tourism books that I read. I want to experience the greatest things on Earth and then share them with others, convincing them to experience them as well. Mum likes to hear about my dream."

"What about your dad?"

"Well, he…he tells me to take days one at a time. Not to get ahead of myself. To let them enjoy the time they have left with me. Well, forget about them. They can tell me what meds to take, what therapy groups to go to, and even tell me I can't leave the house because they're afraid I'll pass out on the street. But they can't take away my imagination. My ability to dream about the future. I won't let them. I can't. Sometimes I think it's all I have."

Rory was shocked. He had never heard Mary talk like this before. Of course, she had her bad days when she couldn't stop throwing up, but she had never condemned her parents or spoke anything against them. He didn't know if this was a new realization she had, if it was the meds altering her mood, or if these were feelings she had been harbouring for years.

"You have me," was all Rory could think to say.

"For how long?" Mary asked, her eyes boring into his.

"For as long as you're alive," Rory replied. "The thing about life, though, Mary, is that it's too short."

"It's long enough," she replied.

Mary shifted herself closer to Rory, leaning her head on his shoulder. He wrapped his arms around her and continued to watch the train until it was out of sight.

"What do you think it would be like?" Mary asked once they could no longer hear the churning of the train.

"To what?" Rory asked. Sometimes she did this. She would be lost in a thought and vocalize it halfway through, leaving everyone else clueless as to what she was talking about.

"I think it would be like jumping off the edge of the world," Mary continued as if she didn't hear him. "And then falling, for what would feel like forever. And then trying to get your bearing but having no earthly idea where you were. And it would be amazing."

Rory stared at her for a minute, still having no idea what she was talking about. But she was so deep in thought, he couldn't bear to pull her out of it. So he continued to hold onto her, afraid if he let go, he would lose her altogether.

Present Day

Rory still was not entirely sure as to how he got Alice and Dex on that train with him. He supposed when they agreed to do it, they weren't convinced that this wasn't a death wish Rory had. He explained why he had to do it. At the time, the others were up for an adventure. Hopping onto the train's car before it pulled out of the station wasn't exactly the hardest task to accomplish. They had simply walked in through the gate, and knew that if anyone asked, they were going to say they were meeting a friend who worked at the station for lunch. Since this wasn't a passenger train, no one was looking for tickets.

The three friends crawled into a car that was carrying steel to god knows where, and within half an hour the train was pulling out from the station.

Once the train started picking up speed, and they realized they were now in the countryside, the three of them understood that the lack of a plan was not doing them any good at the moment. Dex, Alice, and Rory all stood in a row, holding onto a pole for support as they looked at the ground moving at thirty miles an hour. Though the train was going slow, it felt like they were on a speeding bullet.

"So the goal is to land on all fours," Dex said as they plotted their jumping scheme.

"Are you sure?" Alice was the most hesitant of them all but didn't want to miss out on the excitement, so she had agreed to go along with the blokes. She was quickly regretting her decision. "How would you know?"

"I'm a doctor, Alice," Dex said rather pretentiously. "Yeah, a doctor," she replied. "Not a logistics expert!" "That's not even a real profession," Dex retorted.

"I cannot believe I'm going to be the reason we die today." Rory was hating himself for bringing these two with him. He thought he would be a hero to Mary's memory, realizing how much she wanted to do this. He was sure if she were on the train now she would understand what an idiotic idea it was.

"Nobody is dying today!" Dex exclaimed. "We just have to eyeball the right spot, and take that leap of faith."

"Okay," Rory said, trying to sound confident. "So how do we plan to do this? Are we all going at once, or—-"

"I think," Dex said, "logistically speaking-"

"Oh my god, for the last time, you're not a logistics expert!" yelled Alice.

"I was going to say we all need to go one at a time!" Dex yelled back.

"No way!" said Rory, suddenly worried. "You're going to make me go first and then you and Alice will ride off together without me.

It's like the Tube Incident all over again."

"That was completely different," Dex said, looking at Rory. "We were teenagers! We ditched you because we wanted to snog without you hanging around! Look, that doesn't matter right now. We can't all jump at once, or else we'll hit each other on the way down."

"So how do we decide who goes first?" Rory asked. The train was gathering speed.

"I'll go last," Dex offered. "You two will need me to direct you and tell you when to go."

"That's rubbish!" cried Rory. "You go first!"

"Oh shut up, both of you," Alice said to them, letting go of the pole. She steadied herself and moved to the edge of the car.

"What are you doing—-" Dex said, but Alice leaped off the train before he could finish. She landed in the field, tumbling down the hill.

"Oh my god, ALICE!" Dex yelled, and jumped after her.

"This is definitely the Tube Incident all over again," Rory said to himself, and he too jumped out of the train, tumbling down the hill.

The two men lay in the grass on their backs, catching their breath. Alice crawled over to them, helping Rory sit up. The three of them watched as the train pass by.

"Next time you see Mary," Dex said to Rory in between deep breaths, "tell her I hate her."

Rory laughed, working on catching his breath too. His bones

burned with pain, but for once it didn't bother him. The three of them sat there, laughing and groaning until they could no longer see the train.

"I have to tell you all something," Rory said eventually.

Alice gasped sarcastically, "You're not going to tell us you're dying of a terribly fatal disease, are you?" She and Dex laughed.

"I'm being serious, you guys," Rory said. He usually liked it when Alice made light of his situation. It made him feel like he could handle it, like it was more manageable. But something had been weighing on his heart since Mary's funeral. And he was afraid if he didn't tell someone soon, it would suffocate him. He opened his mouth, but nothing came out.

"Rory?" Alice was growing concerned.

"I don't want to die." Rory's words hung in the air. Alice and Dex looked at each other across from Rory, who was in the middle of them.

"Where is this coming from, Ror?" Dex asked his brother.

"I dunno," Rory said quietly.

"Rory, of course you don't want to die," Alice said consolingly. "You're too young."

"No, but the thing is…" Rory wanted them to understand. "The thing is, I'm terrified. I'm absolutely terrified of dying. It's frightening. I don't know what's going to happen. I don't know what it's going to feel like. To take that last, shallow breath of air as the life escapes from me."

"But Rory," Dex couldn't help himself. "You tried to overdose. You tried to kill yourself."

"I was panicked," Rory replied. "I was upset and claustrophobic and needed a way out. I didn't want to die. I just didn't want to exist."

"Rory, please," Alice said, not sure she could handle talk this morbid.

"Please what?" Rory turned to look at her. "Don't talk about it?" He turned to Dex. "Play my sickness off as a joke? I can only do that for so long until it becomes real again. This is happening, you guys. I am dying. And I am so bloody terrified of it...and what's worse, I'm afraid of dying alone."

"What?" Dex said. "Rory, you know Alice and I are here for you.

We're in it 'til the end, mate."

"You two can't be around twenty-four-seven," Rory muttered.

"No, but—-" Dex started.

"And, honestly, I deserve to die alone," Rory interrupted.

"Rory!" Alice was appalled at his behavior. "I don't understand where this is coming from. You've never been self-pitying when it comes to your cancer."

"I'm not feeling sorry for myself," said Rory, exhausted. How could he explain this to them without giving everything away? "I'm simply telling the truth."

"Please, tell me how you dying alone would benefit anyone. Or how you deserve that," Alice prompted.

Rory was silent for a minute. He realized he couldn't keep it in any longer. He turned to his lifelong friend and told her, "Because

I wasn't there for Mary when she died. She was all alone."

Alice and Dex both looked taken aback.

"But...but you told us that you were with her...Mary's parents think you were with her!" Alice exclaimed.

"Yeah, that's because that's what I told them," replied Rory.

"Why?" asked Dex.

"Why?" repeated Rory. "Because I couldn't bear to tell them the truth! How do I tell two people that their only child

81

died alone? A child whom they left in my care, who was my responsibility?"

"How did it happen then?" Alice wanted to know.

"I got a call from the chemist, telling me my prescription was ready," Rory began. He shook his head with disgust at himself. "I told Mary I would wait to get it. But I had been out of my pills for a week. And she could tell it was taking a toll on me. She told me I needed to take care of myself if I was going to take care of her. I should have known better. She was on her bloody death bed for god's sake! And I left her there! All for some damn PILLS!"

His voice echoed throughout the field, but no one else was around. He took a couple of shallow breaths before continuing.

"I came back...I couldn't have been gone more than ten minutes.

I called out to her once I got back to see what she wanted for supper. She hadn't been able to keep anything down for two days. She kept getting sick. But I was going to make her favorite, Cumberland pie. When she didn't answer me, I figured she was sleeping. I went in to wake her up. I bent down to kiss her forehead, the way I always woke her up because she would startle so easily. But when I leaned in—-" his voice hitched, "I didn't hear her breathing. I tried shaking her to get her to wake up, but nothing happened. I checked her pulse, and..." his voice trailed off. The lump in his throat kept him from saying any more.

"Oh, Rory," Alice sighed. Silent tears were streaming down her face.

"Why didn't you tell us, mate?" Dex asked gently.

"I couldn't even come to terms with it myself," admitted Rory. "I hated myself for it. Wouldn't you?" he asked, turning to look at Dex. "Mary and I went through this for ten years, and in the end…

I failed her."

"Is that what you think?" asked Alice. "That you failed her? You just jumped off a train moving forty miles an hour. You stole a bloody pregnancy test for no reason! Except you did have a reason.

Mary. You're doing all these crazy things because she asked you to.

Doing them won't bring her back. But that doesn't matter to you. You're honouring Mary's memory. And in that, you definitely, definitely have not failed her."

Rory shook his head. "No matter how many of these things I can check off her mad list, it doesn't change the fact that I wasn't there for her during the most integral part of our lives together."

"You're right," agreed Dex.

"Dex!" Alice said.

"No, Alice, he's right," Dex continued. "There is no going back to that moment and changing the course of events. Life…It's unpredictable. But, Rory, you could have been in the loo. You could have been on your mobile in another room, or watching the telly! You were there for Mary for ten whole years. Every single day. You left your hometown, your own parents, to be with her every second through her battle. You sacrificed a relationship with Mum and Dad for this girl. She was your life. She was your family. And when it all came to an end…Well, I just don't believe that you were meant to witness that.

And maybe Mary realized it, too."

Rory let that sink in. It was true, Mary never attempted suicide, or tried to run away from him to make his life easier.

There was always an essence about her that he craved for his own life, but he never could point to what it was. Or perhaps he just didn't want to face what he knew it to be.

Rory looked around. "Where the hell even are we?"

"Twenty miles from London?" Alice guessed. "We passed another train station though, about four miles back."

Rory stood up. "Well, then. We better get going if we want to make it back before sundown." He extended his hands to Dex and Alice, helping them up. The three of them began walking the opposite way from the direction the train was going.

"I really thought for a second that you two were pulling the Tube Trick again on me," Rory said, amused.

Alice laughed. "Rory! That was one time! You wouldn't leave us alone, and we wanted to get rid of you!"

"Seriously, mate," Dex said. "You think I would just—-" he ran toward Alice, sweeping her up in his arms-, "steal my girlfriend away and leave you behind? Never!" He ran ahead of Rory, carrying Alice and kissing her, both of them laughing. Rory chuckled to himself and watched them run ahead. He would catch up, he thought to himself. He wanted to give them their moment, though. They did just jump off a train with him, after all.

Seven

A couple of weeks after what the trio would refer to as The Great Train Adventure, Rory had a follow-up doctor's appointment at the hospital. He had gone in with Dex on the tube, but it was up to him to get home. Rory didn't mind. His appointment hadn't exactly lifted his spirits, but it hadn't told him anything he wasn't expecting to hear. His blood levels were worse than a month ago. His white cells were depleting faster than they could replenish themselves, making him more prone to infection every day. It looked like the doctor was right after all: Rory's days were numbered.

Getting his blood drawn usually didn't take a lot out of him, but this time he felt extremely ill afterward. He had refused the biscuit the nurse offered him, but drank the juice. He made his way from St. Bart's to the underground station and found his route. Once he found a seat on the train, he thought, he would be okay. But the tube was busy with people who were coming home from work, and there were no empty seats. Eventually, after several stops, a place opened up. He slumped into it, doing the best he could not to throw up. He breathed in through his nose and out through his mouth, just like Dex had taught them when they were kids. He saw his distorted reflection in the silver pole across from him. He was white as a sheet. He should have eaten the biscuit. He decided that, no matter where the next stop was, he would get off so he could relieve himself.

Sure enough, two minutes later when the tube screeched to a stop, Rory stumbled out and ran to the nearest rubbish bin, retching. Behind him, the doors to the train closed and began to move.

"No," Rory said feebly. He followed the train, knocking on the doors, but to no avail. It took off, leaving him miles from his final destination.

Feeling defeated and increasingly weak, Rory made his way up the stairs from the underground to the pavement, where he figured he would hail a cab. Looking around, he realized he was in Trafalgar Square, and the streets were swarmed with people. It would be impossible to find a taxi cab at this time of day. While attempting (and failing) to hail one, he threw up again on the pavement. This disgusted the bystanders who were also looking for a ride.

"He's drunk," one of them commented to the other. Rory understood how he certainly could have been mistaken for someone intoxicated, seeing as he couldn't see straight due to his lightheadedness and his excessive vomiting.

He began to walk again toward his flat, which was all the way down on Tottenham Court Road, past Leicester Square. This was at least another thirty-minute walk, but he didn't see any other option. He was struggling to keep his balance, knowing if he didn't sit down soon, he would definitely lose consciousness. He found a bench and slumped over the armrest just in time to vomit once more. He pulled out his mobile and dialed, which was quite a feat, given the fact his hands were shaking uncontrollably.

"I need you to come to get me," he mumbled into the receiver.

Thirty minutes later Alice was running down Trafalgar Square, slowing down every few steps only to glance around in the bustle of afternoon foot traffic to see if Rory was among them. She had two bags in her arms, and when she had finally found him curled up on a bench, she slung both onto one shoulder.

"Oh Rory," she breathed. "You look like hell."

Rory looked up at her, his pale complexion making his slight figure look rather ghost-like.

"Come on, let's get you home." Alice hoisted Rory up and walked to the curb with him before she successfully hailed a cab. She ushered him into it, and they rode to their flat.

When they finally got up the stairs, Alice unlocked the door and let Rory in. He felt like he needed to throw up again, but there was nothing left in his stomach.

"Here you are," said Alice. "Go sit on the couch. I'll get some blankets and make you something to eat."

"I'm not hungry," said Rory, collapsing into the couch. He had never felt so relieved to be home.

"I didn't ask if you were, now did I?" Alice was no pushover when it came to Rory's health. Suddenly Rory began to violently dry- heave, his body racked with uncontrollable retching and sobbing.

"Oh," Alice said, rushing to his side. She grabbed the blanket that was thrown over the back of the couch and wrapped it around her friend. She held him and rubbed his arms, trying to suppress his shivering. She knew this was a side effect of the meds he was taking, but it still alarmed her. They sat there like that for over an hour, Rory drifting in and out of consciousness, Alice resting her head on Rory's shoulder, her arms still wrapped tightly around him. They heard the jingling of keys and knew Dex was home. When he entered, Dex looked alarmed at the scene on the couch.

"What happened?" he demanded.

"It hasn't been a good day," Alice explained. And that was all Dex needed to know. He eyed Rory.

"Well…Did you give him his meds? Or did you call Dr. Epstein?" Dex tried to control his tone, but it gave away his vulnerability.

"There's nothing we can do," Alice said. "He's just got the chills and a fever. It's expected at this point, you know that. It's not worth bothering the doctor."

Dex kept his eyes on Rory's pitiful life form. He had seen his brother like this before, he saw people like him every day. But for some reason, Dex had been able to put that out of his mind until now. Finally, he sat down on the other side of Rory, who wasn't attempting to speak, just taking shallow breaths through his mouth. His eyes were drooping, but Dex could tell by the way his eyebrows were furrowed that he was frightened. Dex looked at Alice, who nodded. She gently shifted Rory's weight over to Dex's open arms. Dex held his younger brother, who was still shaking, until eventually, Rory drifted to sleep.

Alice approached Rory hesitantly, holding a steaming mug of tea she had just made. Dex had gone to bed, but Rory was wide awake, looking at an old photo album he had found on the coffee table in the living room. The chill had subsided, and he felt his body temperature returning to its normal state. He had slept for five hours straight, and now that he was up, he couldn't fall back to sleep. Alice curled up next to Rory, looking at the pictures from over his shoulder. She offered him the cup of tea.

"I don't know how much this'll help, but hopefully it relaxes you," Alice offered.

"Thanks," said Rory, accepting it form her.

"Mary leave that for you, too?" Alice asked.

"No," replied Rory. "It's Dex's. It was on the table."

"Dex doesn't let me look at any of his old photographs," said Alice, scanning the pictures from the brothers' childhood. "He's embarrassed or something. Though I can't imagine why, I mean look at the little bugger!" She pointed to a particular picture of Dex, which showed him at four years old in the picture, painting his bare stomach with a paintbrush and purple paint.

"Yes, well, not quite as adorable as this little guy," said Rory, pointing to a picture of himself as a toddler. "I mean, come on. No comparison."

"God, you two were mental as kids." Alice shook her head.

"Especially as teenagers, I remember being the one keeping you two in line."

"Hah," said Rory, "that's a good one."

"What?" said Alice, affronted. "I was definitely the least mad of the three of us."

"Sure you were, Alice," Rory smiled.

Alice sighed. "Well, it's good to know that we didn't change completely."

Rory paused, then looked at her. "Didn't we?" he asked.

Neither of them said anything, and Rory sipped on his tea. After they had flipped through most of the album, Rory spoke.

"Looking through these old photographs reminded me of something. Dex and I used to have a cat. Well, technically it was our mother's. His name was *Mister Flutter*," Rory's voice was coated with contempt. "She had him since before Dex was even born. He was...awful. Really mean to Dex and me. He adored our mum, though. By the time I remember him being around, he was an old grump. But I remember the day he ran away. Dex and I weren't that torn up about it, to be honest, but Mum was quite tearful. I didn't really understand, I was just a little tyke back then. I asked her when Mister Flutter would come home. She told me we would never see him again. You see, cats, when they know they're about to die, tend to run away from home. They go somewhere else so that their owners, the ones who had taken care of them and stuck by them all those years, don't have to watch them die."

Alice had listened intently to Rory this whole time and realized what he was getting at.

"Rory, you're not a cat," she said exasperatedly. "You're not… running away from us, okay?"

Rory looked back at the photo album, and Alice shifted her body so that she was completely facing him.

"Rory," she said, "you need to be here. With us. Dex and I want you here."

Rory looked up at her. "I can't make you two go through what I went through with Mary. Coming home one day to find her… gone. It's better if you get a phone call one day, and that be it."

"A phone call from whom?" Alice said incredulously. "Some random hostel employee who had found that you'd snuffed it in your sleep? No, Rory, that's so ridiculous I can't even believe you're talking about it normally!"

"Alice," he replied, wishing so badly she could just see from his point of view. "I don't want you or Dex seeing what I am becoming."

Alice crossed her arms. "Oh, and what's that precisely?"

"Some helpless life form who sits around drinking tea and looking at photo albums because he's too sick to leave the house!" Rory exclaimed.

"Lots of people do that!" said Alice.

"Yeah, elderly widowed women," said Rory.

Alice took a deep breath. "Look, Rory. You're not going to bail on us, alright? Let us help you. Let us take care of you. We want you here, and if that means taking your good days with your bad, then so be it. We want it all…Besides, how far exactly do you expect to get before

Dex tracks you down and kicks your arse?"

Rory snorted at that and took another sip of tea. "Yeah, I hadn't quite planned that part out yet." He looked back at Alice. "You two really want it all, then?"

Alice looked back at her best friend, her eyes filled with sincerity.

"Yes."

"Alright then," Rory agreed. He handed the photo album to Alice and got up. "I'm off to bed. Cheers." He bent down and kissed her cheek before leaving the living room.

"Goodnight," Alice replied. She watched the blanket trail behind him as he left. She heard his door close and looked back at the photo album. The page was turned to a particular picture that Alice remembered too well. It was of her and Rory the morning of one of their first days of high school. Alice's hair was in a high ponytail, her skirt hiked up more than was allowed by the school dress code. Her nose was pierced with a diamond stud that she hadn't worn in years. Rory's hair was longer and quite a mess, as he was always neglecting to comb it. His shirt was untucked, and his tie was hanging loosely around his neck. The two of them had their backpacks on one shoulder and were smiling impatiently at the camera.

Fall, 2004

Alice and Rory both blinked as the camera flashed. Alice was wishing Rory had come to pick her up now, rather than vice versa.

She was just grateful that her parents weren't into this sort of send-off. Neither of them even remembered she started back to school today, anyway. Not that she had expected them to.

"Just one more!" Sarah exclaimed as she refocused the camera.

"Mum, I think we got it, alright?" Rory said impatiently. "Can we go before we're late?"

Sarah lowered the camera, her smile faltering slightly. "Yes… alright, let me just go and get you the lunch I packed for you." She scurried past Arthur and Dex, who were having a conversation of their own as she ran inside the house. Rory rolled his eyes. Alice turned to face Rory. "Alright, you. Out with it."

"Out with what?" Rory was confused.

"Why is your mum insisting on taking photos?" Alice wanted to know. "Your mum never takes photos. And you've barely said a word to me all morning. Are you thinking of ditching me this term? Because if so, good luck finding someone who will listen to you ramble on and on about all of your absurd obsessions like—-"

"No, no, I'm not angry at you, Alice. Just—-" Rory took her elbow and pulled her away, out of Dex and Arthur's earshot. "I've got to tell you something. But you have got to swear you won't tell anyone. Not at school, your parents, anyone. Can you keep a secret?"

"Of course," Alice agreed. "You already know mine." She nodded in the direction where Dex was still talking with his father.

"Right," said Rory, taking a deep breath. "Well, Mum took me to the hospital the other day for a couple of blood tests. Because you know, I haven't been feeling all that well lately. Well, the blood tests led to bone scans, and the bone scans led to…Well, it turns out…" His voice trailed off, and he looked at his feet.

"Well?" asked Alice, who was growing concerned. "Spit it out,

Rory."

Rory looked up at her. "I've got cancer?"

Alice's eyes grew wide and she looked taken aback. "Wait, are you saying it like a question? As in you may have cancer?"

Rory shook his head. "No, no I've…I've actually got cancer. Sorry."

Alice didn't know how to process this. She looked back at Dex and Arthur, who were laughing and carrying on their own conversation.

How could they be carrying on like that if they knew Rory had cancer?

"Oh my god, Rory," was all Alice could think to say. "Is it serious? Like can you die from it?"

"Well, it's called osteosarcoma," said Rory. "Basically I have bone cancer. But it's in its early stages, so apparently that might be a good sign? I don't…I don't really know, we have an appointment to talk with a specialist on Tuesday. Look, just don't get upset, alright?

There's a reason I trust you with this."

Alice, whom Rory had never seen cry, was suddenly fighting back tears with every nerve in her body.

"Rory," she said, "my best mate—- my only mate—— just told me he has cancer, and you expect me not to get upset?"

"Shh," pleaded Rory. "Just keep your voice down, okay? Every time I mention it in front of Mum, she starts crying."

Just then Sarah re-emerged from the house, blowing her nose, carrying Rory's lunch. "Here you are, dear," she handed the lunch to her son, kissing him on the forehead. He let her.

"Thanks, Mum," he replied.

"Alright, off you go, you two." Sarah shooed them on their way to school. Alice was still looking at Rory in shock. Sarah, who saw this, asked her, "Alice, you alright there, dear? You look ill."

"No, it's fine…I'm not ill," she replied, trying her best to recover.

"Let's go, Al," Rory grabbed her wrist and began to drag her away from the scene. What seemed like the first time since she had arrived at the Gallaghers' home, Dex noticed her.

"Cheers, you two," he called. "Don't do anything I ever did!"

But, for once, Alice didn't pay attention to Dex or acknowledge his witty remark. She merely stared at Rory as they walked, who in turn stared straight ahead, avoiding her gaze.

Eight

Dex stepped out of the shower and wrapped a towel around his waist. He shook his hair with his hands and let it fall back over his face. He opened the medicine cabinet to look for his aftershave. Dex and Alice were going on their first date in a while. Neither of them seemed to be on the same nocturnal schedule, and when they were, Rory was usually the subject of concern. Not tonight, though. Tonight it was all about Alice, he would make sure of that.

He didn't know why he was so nervous. Perhaps because it had been a while since they had spent time just the two of them. He had no secrets from her, but she still made him feel edgy at times when he knew he needed to impress her. It had been the three of them now for so long that just being alone with Alice scared him a bit. He didn't want it to be like those nights out that new parents went on to get away from their children, only to find themselves talking about their children the entire time. He knew Rory wasn't his or Alice's child, but that didn't keep it from feeling that way sometimes.

His hands were shaking so hard that he actually ended up knocking some of the medicine bottles out of the cabinet.

"Dammit," he muttered. He didn't want Alice to notice how on edge he was. He couldn't help but keep remembering Rory's story of how Mary died while he was at the chemist. Rory was fine now – well, as fine as someone with a deteriorating illness could be – but he knew as well as anyone who had ever dealt with cancer that it was a sneaky bastard.

He bent down to pick up the three bottles he had knocked off the shelf, all of them Rory's. However, when he picked them up, they felt fuller than they should have. Upon further examination, Dex concluded that Rory hadn't been taking any of the medications for at least a week. With growing fury, he began rummaging through the rest of the tiny bottles in the cabinet until he collected all five of Rory's. None of them, including morphine for pain, had been touched for days.

Towel still wrapped around his waist, Dex stormed out of the bathroom and into Rory's room. When he entered, Rory was lying in bed as per usual, reading a book. He glanced up at Dex when he entered, annoyed at the interruption.

"No need to knock," he said sarcastically.

Instead of responding, Dex held up the bottles of pills.

"Oh," Rory said uncomfortably. "Look, Dex, I can explain."

"Yes," yelled Dex, "please explain to me how these bottles I got filled for you a week ago are still filled to the brim!"

"What were you doing prying through my things?" Rory shot back defensively.

"It fell, and I picked it up. Don't try to avoid the question!"

"What question? Oh, you mean this interrogation? I could try to explain my reasoning to you, but you wouldn't understand! You would never understand how those pills make me feel."

"Rory, I'm a doctor. I am fully aware of the side effects."

"Yes, Doctor," Rory sneered, "but you don't know the toll they take on a person! The effects they have on me! I can hardly will myself to get on the tube to go to the hospital for my appointments because I'm afraid I'll be sick everywhere. Remember what happened just last week? I get panic attacks when I have to do the shopping because I'm afraid I'll lose it in public And the daze…" He closed his eyes and shook his head. "Oh, the daze is the worst. Sometimes I feel like I'm not even here. Days can go by, and I feel like no time has passed at all. Or maybe, in fact, an eternity has. I can't go on like this, Dex. Please don't make me take them." Rory's eyebrows wrinkled in his plea.

Dex stared at his little brother, who was quite literally begging him for mercy. He realized the power that he held over his little brother. The power he held over him since they were kids. Suddenly he was ten years old again, Rory seven. The two brothers were wrestling, and Dex had Rory in a headlock. Rory's laughing had abruptly turned to screaming and crying. 'Too hard, Dex! Stop! Please!'

Dex cleared his throat. "These pills…they're breaking you down then."

"Every day," replied Rory.

"But so does the cancer."

"I would rather live my last days being fully present with you and Alice, even if they were cut short, if it meant giving up the daze, fatigue, and nausea caused by the meds. I want to experience the things Mary has planned for me. I want to be alive – fully alive – until I'm simply…not."

Dex looked down at the five different bottles he was still clutching in his palms. He unexpectedly thrust all of them at the wall, the containers busting and pills raining onto the floor. Rory, startled, got out of bed. Dex strode over to him, his face contorted. He silently put his hand on his brother's shoulder, squeezing it tightly. He nodded at him. Then, without another word, he turned around and walked out of his room, closing the door. He made a silent promise to Rory not to tell Alice.

Spring, 2005

As per the usual routine after school, Rory and Alice were hanging out in Rory's bedroom. Rory leaned against the head of his bed while Alice lay perpendicular to him at the foot, on her stomach. They were both poring over brochures that had been given to them by their teachers at school, insisting that it was time for them to begin thinking about their future careers. As Rory rubbed his bald head, he wasn't thinking much about his future unless it involved Mary, but didn't want to miss out on the fun with Alice.

"I cannot believe our homework is to choose the career we'll have for the rest of our lives," Alice exclaimed scornfully, flipping her high ponytail over her shoulder. "We're only sixteen! I mean, this is a major turning point in our lives. It's what we'll be committed to for the next fifty years!"

"If we're lucky," Rory said absentmindedly, looking through the schooling requirements to become a phlebotomist.

Alice looked over her shoulder at him. "Oh, please. Don't go feeling sorry for yourself like that." She turned back to her pamphlet. "You don't think I've earned that right?" Rory inquired.

"Nope."

Rory grinned slightly. "But you'll tell me when I have, right?"
"Of course I will," Alice replied, still not looking up.

Finally, she turned to him. "Just not today." She smiled. After a while looking through the options for career paths, she finally spoke.

"Maybe I could be a teacher."

Rory snorted. Alice acted affronted. "What?"

"Alice, you hate school."

"True," she agreed. "But I like kids. I could teach primary school or something."

"Yeah but to be a teacher you actually have to know stuff."

"Watch it, you, I'm clever!"

"Yeah? Then why don't you show anybody?"

"It's none of their business."

Rory laughed at her. She threw a pillow at him.

"Alright then, you prat, what do you want to be when you grow up?" she challenged him.

"Oh Alice, you talk as though I'm going to live through qualifications."

Alice sat up straight, turning toward him. "Seriously, Ror. Say you absolutely had to choose something you were going to do for the rest of your life, and you were going to live forever. What would

it be?"

Rory sighed and stared out of his window. It was a dreary day, but then again, most days were dreary in York. There was one person who brought a splash of color with her wherever she went, but Rory didn't see her outside his window. Not yet, anyhow.

After several moments of silence, Rory finally answered. "I'd like to be a husband."

"A husband?" Alice said, disbelievingly.

"It's no more ridiculous than your teacher idea!" Rory cried defensively, immediately regretting letting a sensitive aspect of himself slip out.

"No, Rory, I'm not judging," she assured him. "I'm just surprised, that's all. I mean, this is coming from the bitter guy who hates puppies. I mean come on, who hates puppies?"

"I do not hate puppies, I just dislike all animals."

"Whatever. So, anyone in particular's husband? Or just some random girl's?"

Rory shook his head. "Not some random girl's. Mary's."

Alice looked excited. "Really? Mary's? I had no idea you two were so serious!"

Rory was quickly regretting every word that came out of his mouth. He couldn't say anything to Alice without her making a big deal out of it. "I mean, I don't know where she stands, but I know where I do."

"Wait," Alice held up her hand. "You want to marry this girl, and I haven't even met her yet?"

"I'm not letting you meet her."

"Why not?" Alice asked, offended. "Because you're mad."

"Well, I won't be, around her! Please, Rory, I have to meet the girl who has softened my best friend's stone of a heart. This is incredible!"

"Mmmm, no." Rory glanced at his watch. "Which reminds me, you better be off."

"Wait, why?"

"Because Mary is coming over, and I rather you not make one of your lasting impressions on her."

"Mary is coming here!?" Alice squealed.

"Yes," Rory said, impatiently. "So if you would please show yourself out—-"

The sound of the doorbell cut Rory off.

"Oh my god!" Alice leaped off the bed and rushed out of the bedroom.

"Wait! Alice!" Rory called after her, following as quickly as his stiff joints would allow.

But Alice, with her body made of cancer-less cells, was too quick for Rory. She hopped over the last four stairs and wrenched open the door. She found herself standing face to face with Mary, whose arm was up, just about to knock on the door.

"Hi, Mary!" Alice exclaimed.

"Hello, stranger who knows my name," Mary replied, lowering her arm. "I'm sorry, have we met?"

Rory staggered up behind Alice. "Mary, I'm so sorry," he huffed, out of breath. "This is Alice. She was just leaving."

"Oh, Alice!" Mary said, understanding dawning on her. "Alice Who Works at the Fair!"

"I do," Alice replied.

"Yeah, Rory's mentioned you a couple of times."

"All good things, I hope."

"Yeah," Rory chimed in, "I decided not to scare her with the truth."

Alice threw Rory a look of disdain over her shoulder. "Well," she said to Mary, "I guess I'll just let you two get on with...you know."

From behind her, Rory rolled his eyes. Mary smiled at him and then at Alice, who looked as though she was using every ounce of self-control to keep something inside of her.

Unfortunately, she was unable to contain herself.

"Ahhhhh!" she burst out, throwing her arms around Mary and jumping up and down, all the while embracing her.

Rory came to Mary's rescue, untangling Alice from her neck. He handed Alice her book bag, which he had brought down with him as he chased after her.

"Alright then, Alice, off you go," he said warningly.

"Bye!" Alice chirped as she skipped down the steps to the

road. When she was halfway down the sidewalk, she turned back and blew a kiss to the couple. Mary waved back at her and stepped inside Rory's house, closing the door behind her.

"Is she always like that?" she asked as she unlaced her boots.

"Afraid so," Rory nodded, taking her coat.

"A girl could get jealous you know."

Rory snickered. "Of Alice? I know no one who could possibly be jealous of Alice."

"But she is your best friend."

"Yeah, well," Rory led Mary upstairs. "Ours is the kind of friendship that forms from putting two people together who are too good for this world." They reached his bedroom. "How are you?" He kissed her on the cheek.

"Fine, now that I'm here with you," Mary blushed. Rory smiled.

"Well come on in." And with that, Rory closed his bedroom door.

Present Day

Alice lay in bed, wide awake. Supper had been lovely, and Dex surprised her with tickets to a West End theatre to see a new, independent play Alice's co-worker was in. They hadn't gotten back until well past midnight, and Dex went straight to sleep. He was on call from six in the morning, so he was taking full advantage of what little sleep he could get. However, Alice's weekend began the next day and she had a hard time motivating herself to try and rest, as her mind was swimming with a million thoughts. Dex and Alice had hardly spoken about Rory at all the entire night, and she had to admit that it was a nice break. However, now that she was home, and reality was just in the next room, she realized how easily her world could

102

come crashing down around her.

She wasn't sure how she was supposed to handle Rory's death when it came. She had known him since they were both children, after all. But Dex was his brother. And she would need to be a support for him. But who would be there for her?

Alice slowly crawled out of bed, careful not to wake Dex. She needn't have worried, though, as Dex could sleep through Armageddon. She tiptoed across the floor, cringing as it creaked. She glanced over her shoulder at her bedmate, who hadn't so much as stirred. Alice quietly opened the door and leaned it shut behind her. She crept down the hall to Rory's bedroom. When she saw the light was on from under the door, she lightly tapped on it with her knuckles.

"Come in," she heard from inside. She opened the door quietly. Rory was sitting up in bed, looking tired and pale, but otherwise content. He was reading a book.

"Hi," she said, standing in the doorway.

"Hey there," said Rory, putting his book on the bedside table. "I thought I was the only one up at this hour."

Alice sat down at the foot of his bed. "Dex is asleep. I couldn't though."

"No?" Rory propped his pillows up behind him and sat up a bit straighter.

"Mhmm…" she pulled her knees up under her chin. "Rory? I need to talk to you about something. But it's hard for me. Because I'm not good at real talk."

"Sorry?" asked Rory, confused.

"I don't like real talk," repeated Alice. "I'm a primary school teacher. I live in a world of glitter and imagination. I don't have real talk on a regular basis because I'm conversing with five-year-old children for most of the day. And I don't like talking about your illness with Dex because it's easier just to make things funny or play it off as not so serious. But this is serious."

"Alright…" Rory said, growing concerned.

Alice began breathing quickly and shallowly. "Okay, so the thing is…don't die."

"Excuse me?"

"Don't die. You can't." She was speaking very quickly now. "Because honestly, besides Dex, you are my best friend. We've known each other forever. You're Dex's brother, but you're also my person.

You are the person whom I told when I first fancied Dex. You are the one who told Dex to ask me to move in with him. You're the reason we're together. You're our Third. Not like a third wheel, either. Just…a third. What are we going to do without you?"

Rory looked thoughtfully at his friend for a while. Alice was not a fragile girl, yet he knew whatever words he chose next would either comfort or break her.

"Here's the thing," he began. "We don't get to choose the people we meet. Sure, we can choose our friends. And, in a sense, we can choose who our family is. But we cannot choose the people we meet. For some reason, I met you. And I liked you enough to keep you around. And to set you up with my brother. And to surrender to your care when I became this poor life form."

They both laughed softly at that. Alice's laughter turned to tears though, and she found herself trying to control her breathing. She didn't want to wake Dex in the other room with her crying.

"My point is," Rory continued, leaning toward her, "I'm glad that I met you. But we have to bid farewell to the people we meet at some point. It might be the day we meet them. It could be a couple of months, or it could be years. And fortunately for me, I get to wait my entire lifetime before saying goodbye to you and Dex."

Alice wiped her nose with her sleeve. "I refuse to take comfort in the fact that you're dying young."

Rory shook his head. "I'm not asking you to. Alice, I died the day Mary did. I stopped living when I knew she had taken her last breath. And then Mary, in her infinite nerve, tried to bring me back to life with these letters. Reminders, if you will, of everything we were together, and everything we weren't. And it has worked. But it was a plaster on a hemorrhage. We can't deny the inevitable. And I can't be your Third anymore, when I was always Mary's One."

Alice sniffled. "But there are still letters left, still things for you to do," she said in a small voice.

"And we'll get it done," Rory insisted. He took Alice's hand.

"Alice, you and Dex are going to thrive. One day you will get married. And you will have a beautiful child. And that child will have the two most amazing parents he could ask for. And you won't need me around any more. You'll have a real child to take care of."

"You're not our child, Rory."

"Aren't I?"

Alice averted her eyes.

"Look, I'm not angry about it," insisted Rory. "Because I know that you aren't. I just need you to know that I will be at peace. And I hope you can find your own in that."

By now Alice was openly crying, not caring who she woke.

"But...but who am I going to complain about Dex to when

he puts a red sock in the whites when doing the washing, or when he adds too much salt to the pasta, or when he forgets his wallet, and I have to bring it to him at the hospital?

Rory chuckled. "You can still complain to me. I'll be listening, just like I know Mary still hears me."

Alice couldn't say another word, she was sobbing so hard. She put her hand over her mouth to stifle the sound. She moved to the other side of Rory's bed and lay down next to him, and he wrapped an arm around her. She lay there, weeping into his shoulder until the two of them drifted into oblivion.

Nine

Alice woke up that next morning and stumbled back to her and Dex's room. This was not the first time the two friends had shared a bed together; they had sleepovers all the time in primary school. Even after they hit puberty, Alice and Rory always spent the night at the other's house after a late night of partying. Both were secure in their platonic relationship, and last night had been no different.

Dex was already getting dressed and ready for work when Alice entered the room. He turned around as he put on his tie.

"You sneaked out on me last night," he said.

"I couldn't sleep, and I needed to talk to Rory," Alice replied, crawling back under her covers.

"I get that," said Dex, knotting the tie at the base of his neck. "But you know you can always talk to me too, right?"

"I know," Alice said quietly, turning on her side to face the opposite wall. Dex came over to her and crawled onto his side of the bed. He leaned over and spoke softly in her ear.

"I know he's your friend just as much as he is my brother, Al." Alice pursed her lips together, fighting back tears. She nodded. Dex got up and left for work, and she let her mind drift off until she was asleep again.

The siren woke Alice with a start. At least, that's what she thought it was. For a moment she couldn't breathe. She clasped her chest, and she didn't realize what had woken her up at first. But then she heard it again, and this time she knew it wasn't a siren. It was Rory.

She bounded out of bed and raced to Rory's room. She whipped the door open, revealing her friend writhing in pain on his bed, whom she had left sleeping calmly not two hours before. He was clutching the side of his stomach and dry-heaving over the edge of his bed.

"Rory!" Alice yelled, alarmed at what she was witnessing. "Rory, what happened?" She marched over to him and kneeled at the bedside.

"It hurts," he moaned. "What does?"

"My legs and chest. They hurt so badly it's making me ill. And last night Dex threw my morphine out because I wasn't taking any."

Alice groaned. Rory was in pain, and the one thing that was going to help was no longer an option.

"But Dex can call in a new prescription," Alice said, soothingly.

"But I need it now!" Rory cried. "Alice, I need Dex, go and get him, please go and get him."

"Ror, Dex is at work," Alice replied, helpless. "He'll be home later, but I don't know what he can do for you except getting you more morphine."

"I don't want morphine I want…something that won't make me… forget everything…Aghhhhh!" He began gasping for air, pointing to his chest. "I can't breathe! I can't…I can't breathe!"

Alice grasped Rory's hand with her own and placed the other one on his shoulder. "Rory, it's alright. Take slow, deep breaths, okay? Here, prop up." She helped shift Rory's weight up in bed and leaned him against his pillows. "It will help you breathe better. You're panicking. I'm going to phone Dex, alright?" She turned to go get her mobile.

"No," Rory cried, grabbing her arm. "Alice, don't leave me. I'm going to die, Alice-I'm-going-to-die!"

Rory reached out for her, but she had left. Rory stared at the ceiling, trying to focus on it and not the sharp stab he felt in his left leg. He grimaced, trying not to scream while simultaneously trying to control the rise and fall of his chest. Alice rushed back into the room, her mobile to her ear.

"It's me," he heard her say as he closed his eyes. "Rory's run out of his pain medication, and he's panicking. He's in a lot of pain, and I don't know what to do. What should I do, call nine-nine-nine?"

"I can get him another bottle of morphine and bring it home," Dex said from the other end. "I'll just get someone to cover me while I'm gone."

"Are you sure?" Alice looked over at Rory.

"Yeah, I would get there before the paramedics anyway," Dex replied. "Tell Rory to hold on, I'll be there before he knows it."

"Okay, I will. I love you." She hung up.

"What...did...he...say?" Rory choked.

"He said he'll be here with more morphine soon." Alice tossed her phone on the nightstand. "Until then, you just have to wait it out. I'm so sorry, Ror. I know it's hard, but a lot of this is just you losing your nerve, so try to relax, okay?"

"I can't, Alice, I can't," Rory sobbed.

"Right, it's alright," soothed Alice, thinking quickly. "Er... where are Mary's letters?"

Rory pointed to the drawer in his nightstand. She opened it and took out the only item in it — the envelope containing the letters from Mary. She rummaged through the manila envelope until she found the one numbered 4.

"Here we are." She crawled onto the opposite side of the bed from where Rory was lying. She put an arm around him, rubbing his shoulder as she showed him the envelope. Rory leaned his head on her shoulder, taking shallow breaths. He tried to control himself, but the shaking overtook his body before he could. Alice kept a firm arm around him as she opened the envelope and began to read aloud Mary's words:

Dear Rory,

There's never a bad day for a fair, is there? That's what my dad used to say when he would take me when I was younger. Do you remember the day you took me? You asked me what my favourite thing to do was. You rolled your eyes when I told you it was go to the fair. But you took me anyway, for our first anniversary of dating. Although, to be fair, we had done a lot more than most people do before their first date. I like to use the excuse I always store in my back pocket of "we were on a time crunch." Of course, that didn't fly so well with my parents when they walked in that time. But of course, that's a different memory altogether. I remember our day at the fair so well. It was the first day it hadn't rained in weeks. The sun was beaming down on us, and we were surrounded by people who were laughing, enjoying themselves, and just having a good time. It was as if the universe had, for once, been on our side.

Fall, 2005

York held fairs year-round; it was one of the things for which the city was known. Rory and Mary had walked there. He picked her up at seven sharp, intent on not being late. They two of them were lost in the fresh air, taking in the sights and smells. Rory had been to chemotherapy that day, and the poison had recently robbed him of his hair. He donned a knit cap to protect his bald head against the chilled wind that interrupted the otherwise perfect weather. Neither of them was thinking about this, though. Their minds were far from it. Instead, they were walking hand in hand, smiling from ear to ear, walking with excitement toward the lights illuminating the way to the fun.

"Whoa," was all Rory could manage, taking it all in.

"I know!" cried Mary.

When the two of them reached the ticket booth, Rory pulled out twenty pounds. "Two tickets please," he told the attendant.

"So, what do you want to do first?" Mary asked him once they had gotten their tickets.

"I don't know," Rory said honestly. "It's up to you." "Well, what's your favorite game?" she asked.

"Don't have one," Rory shrugged. "Your favorite ride?"

He shrugged again.

"Oh my god, Rory Gallagher." Mary looked at him with astonishment. "Are you a virgin to the York Fair?"

Rory laughed sheepishly.

"Didn't your parents ever bring you here as a kid?" Mary wanted to know, as they began walking toward the rides and booths.

"Not really," replied Rory. "I mean, they took my brother when he was little. We never had the time or money to do stuff like this as kids though."

"Well then," Mary said, straightening up. "I will just have to guide you through this night!" They looked around at all the kids shrieking in delight as they ran from ride to ride.

"Oh!" Mary yelped. She had seen the sledgehammer game and the ultimate prize for the contestant who scored the highest. It was a giant stuffed bear that was half the size of Mary, easily.

"I want that," she said, pointing to the toy.

Rory looked over to where she was pointing, his smile faltering once he saw what the game entailed. He hadn't told her that he had had chemotherapy that day. He knew she would think he wasn't up for anything, and that wasn't true at all. He took her hand, and they ran over to the game.

"Step on up, mate," the man running the game invited Rory. "Win a prize for the pretty lady."

Rory approached the scale. He picked up the sledgehammer off the ground. The simple weight of it made him light-headed. Nevertheless, he swung it over his shoulder and hit the scale, causing the marker to go halfway to the top. Rory grunted, dropped the hammer, and grabbed his knees as he bent over to catch his breath.

"That's alright, have another go!" cried the employee.

Rory looked back at Mary, who gave him an encouraging smile.

He smiled back at her and picked up the sledgehammer once more.

"Whoo! Go Rory!" Mary cheered.

By this time, a line had formed behind Rory, and a few men were waiting to impress their dates with their strength. When Rory hit the scale this time, the marker only rose a quarter of the way up.

"Never mind, maybe next time then," said the employee.

"One more time," Rory said.

Mary watched nervously as Rory tried again. He steadied

himself, took a deep breath, and swung one more time, crying out in pain as it feebly hit the scale.

"One more time!" Rory pleaded.

"Give it up, mate," said one of the guys behind him. "It's someone else's turn."

"Sorry chum," agreed the employee. "You gotta go. Maybe another time."

Rory looked defeated at the man, then down at the hammer. He dropped it on the ground. Mary came up to him at that moment, grabbed his arm, and pulled him out of the line.

"Alright, who's next?" Rory heard the man call out as they walked away.

"Don't worry about it," Mary insisted. "I don't even know where I'd put a stuffed animal that big. He'd take up my entire bed!"

Rory shook his head. "I dunno what happened. I guess I'm not as strong as I thought."

"You had chemo this week, didn't you?" Mary asked.

Rory avoided her question at first. Then, "Yeah," he said.

"Why didn't you mention it? We didn't have to go out tonight."

"No, no, I'm feeling fine. Look, it's just taking a toll on this otherwise perfectly sculpted body."

They laughed as they continued to walk. Rory put his arm around Mary, a gesture that had become so natural after the past twelve months that neither of them really thought about it any more.

"Alice is working one of the booths this year," Rory said. "Maybe we'll see her. She's been bringing my assignments lately, but otherwise, I don't see her much."

"You and Alice are awfully close, you know," Mary observed, but she was smiling. "A girl could wonder things."

"Don't be getting jealous on me, now," Rory said, smiling. "She fancies my brother, which is undoubtedly the true reason she's at my house so often."

"I thought Dex was much older."

"He is. Which is why he doesn't pay much attention to her, poor thing. It keeps me from having to fetch my books, though, so I let her do it."

"You're horrible," Mary laughed. She knew he was only trying to make her feel less threatened by Alice. It didn't take much for Mary to feel inferior to other girls her age. By sixteen years old, she should have had more curves and be able to fill out her clothes a lot better than she did. But her cancer had stolen (among other things) any sort of feminine feature she could flaunt. Most jeans were too big for her, so she relied on dresses and skirts with jumpers, which engulfed her slight figure. Her chemotherapy had stolen her hair a long time ago, and it had just recently begun to grow out again. Lately, she styled it in the same pixie every day.

The two of them did everything they could think of that night: They ate cotton candy until they felt ill, went on rides until they were sure they would get sick, and even went on the York Festival's famous ferris wheel, called the Big Wheel. Rory had not, until now, had reason to divulge his deathly fear of heights to Mary. He kept his mouth closed the entirety of the ride, and not only to keep from letting her in on his secret. He was confident he was going to throw up. His head was still spinning after the ride was over, when Mary dragged him over to a tent labeled Psychic.

"Oop!" she said when they reached it. "Only one at a time it says, I suppose you'll wait out here for me?" She looked up at him with a twinkle in her eyes.

Rory wasn't keen on wasting time at a psychic. Being raised by his parents, he always relied on logic and fact. Aware of Mary's religious upbringing, he didn't understand why she would even bother with a psychic.

"Because it's just for fun," Mary said.

"Yeah but, you've always said that sort of stuff is witchcraft." "I don't take what they say seriously, Rory," Mary laughed.

"Okay, but you're not going in there to try to…convert anyone, are you?"

"Ha, ha, of course not, I'll be back in a few minutes." And off Mary went into the tent.

Rory waited outside the tent for ten minutes. He crossed his arms and leaned against one of the wooden posts, watching as teenagers his age walked by, laughing and carrying on. When Mary finally emerged, she had a solemn look on her face.

"Did you get the answers you were looking for, then?" Rory asked in a mystical voice.

"Don't mock me, Rory," Mary said, but she was smiling.

"Seriously, though, what did you ask her?" Rory wanted to know.

"That's none of your business!" she replied.

"Fine, fine," Rory conceded. "I'll drop it. It's all bollocks anyway."

"Not always," Mary said simply. She began walking toward the food stands. It was the first time in a while she had been hungry, and she was fully intent on taking advantage of it. Rory sighed and followed her. He bought the two of them a bag of popcorn and leaned against one of the posts as they ate. Mary started to laugh, remembering something.

"I can't believe you almost puked on that kid after riding the Fireball," she said chuckling. "And the Big Wheel."

"I'd like to blame it on the chemo, but honestly I just don't think I can do roller coasters," Rory laughed.

"Mary?" a voice asked from behind them.

Mary and Rory turned around to find themselves facing a boy about their age. His broad shoulders filled out the t-shirt he was wearing.

"Alexander!" she called back, surprised. She gave him a hug. "I haven't seen you in months! Are you here with Harmony?"

"No, no, just some of my mates," Alexander said. "She misses you though, never seen my sister so upset in her life, poor girl. I bet you anything you were her only friend at school."

"Oh, that's not true," Mary said, shaking her head. She felt a pang of undue guilt in her chest.

"At school?" Rory asked pointedly.

"Oh, Alex, I'm so sorry. This is Rory." She indicated to Rory. "We go to group therapy together. It's like a support group for people with cancer."

"Oh, so you've got it too, then?" Alexander asked Rory. Rory just stared at him.

"Yeah," Mary finally spoke for Rory. "Well, a different type. But yeah."

"So when are you coming back to school, Mare?" Alexander asked Mary. "We miss you there!"

"Ha ha," Mary laughed nervously. "Well, that's the inconvenient part about the whole cancer thing. It doesn't really care about school or friends, or life for that matter."

"Well, you look like you're doing well," said Alexander, with a tone indicating he was looking for an exit from the conversation.

Mary noticed he was eyeing her pixie haircut. "I can't wait to tell Harmony I saw you, she'll freak. Come over soon, okay?"

"I will, thanks Alex," Mary said, giving him an out.

Alexander nodded at Rory. "You take care too, mate. Nice to meet you."

"Yeah," replied Rory as Alexander rejoined his group of alpha males.

"Alexander and I went to school together," Mary explained to Rory, resuming eating the popcorn she was holding. "Before my parents took me out, that is. Our mums are in a Bible Study together."

Rory didn't seem to hear her. They were standing near where they had come in, and the sledgehammer game was only a few feet away.

Rory took off toward it without a single word.

"Rory?" Mary was caught off guard by Rory's sudden departure. "Rory, where are you going?" She threw the half-empty bag of popcorn in the nearest bin and trotted off after him. She watched as he cut the line and took the hammer from a person who had scored high. People in the queue were still cheering as Rory grabbed the hammer and took his position.

"Oi! There's a queue, mate!" the man running the game shouted at Rory. But Rory didn't listen. With every ounce of strength he could muster, he swung the hammer over his shoulder and slammed it on the scale.

Ding!

He won the giant stuffed bear. "Yes!" He fist-pumped the air. Beaming, he turned around to face Mary, but she was storming off toward the exit. He dropped the hammer and began to limp after her, grunting in pain.

"Mary! Mary, wait!" he called after her. When at last he caught up with her, he took her wrist and spun her around.

"What was that?" he demanded.

"*What was that?*" Mary gestured to the game.

"What are you talking about?" Rory panted, trying to catch his breath.

"Why did you get the sudden urge to prove your strength?" she cried. "You weren't bothered with it before."

"Before what?" Rory asked, but he knew she was right.

"Before we ran into Alexander!" she exclaimed. "Admit it, you saw me being friendly with another guy and it made you jealous."

"I am not jealous of Alexander," Rory spat.

"Perhaps not," huffed Mary, crossing her arms, "but you think you're inferior to him, don't you?"

Rory opened his mouth to retort and immediately regretted what began spurting from his mouth. It didn't stop him though.

"So what if I did? I saw the way Alex looked at you, and the way he looked at me. And I know what he saw, Mary. He saw a scrawny, little, sick kid who is supposed to be this incredible girl's boyfriend. And so yeah! I feel inferior. Unworthy, even!" He avoided her gaze after his outburst, staring shamefully at the ground.

Mary stared at him, fuming. "Well, fine, then! But if you think you are substandard compared to Alex, and everyone else who doesn't have a single, bloody cancer cell in their body, then you're saying the same about me. And I refuse to think like that. I can't afford to, Rory! You call yourself unworthy? You're calling me unworthy too! Don't think for a second that I don't get jealous either."

Rory looked up and met her gaze.

"There's a reason Alexander and his sister haven't seen me in months," Mary continued. "It's because I cannot even bear going over to their house and being the odd one out. The sick one, as you so elegantly put it." Angry tears were streaming down her face, but she ignored them.

Rory didn't say anything for a while. He looked up at the stars above them. He thought he saw a shooting one, but it was going too slowly. It was a plane, he decided. How beautiful it must be, to be all the way up there, and have no choice but to not worry about the problems that plagued you when you were on solid ground.

"I'm sorry," Rory said somberly, still staring at the airplane pass overhead.

"Yeah. Well." Mary hastily wiped her cheeks. "You should be. You shouldn't have done that to yourself," she indicated behind Rory at the hammer game. "Are you okay?"

Rory gingerly massaged his left shoulder with his right hand. "I will be." After a pause, "We should go and get you that stuffed bear. I nearly died trying to win it for you. The least you could do is accept it."

Rory was aware that this attempt at playful banter was a risk, but Mary caved as the corners of her lips curved upward into the faintest of smiles. They began to walk back to the counter to collect their prize.

"You're an idiot, you know," Mary said.

"So I've been told," Rory replied, wrapping his arm around her.

Rory caught Mary's eye as she looked up at him, and they both realized they were in the middle of a moment. These, thought Rory, these were the moments that he wanted to live in forever. If he could just stop time right then and there, and there they would exist for eternity. In this place of mutual circumstance, yet equal hopefulness. Neither mortal nor immortal, they were simply existing. But they were existing together, and that's all

Rory ever could have wished for.

Present Day

Rory's breathing was even, now. Alice was staring at him intently, and he wished she wouldn't. It made him uncomfortable, like he was being observed under a microscope. He had felt that way often, ever since he was diagnosed. Nurses kept drawing blood, lab technicians running tests, and doctors avoiding eye contact as they reported results. What if this was just one big experiment, Rory had thought once or twice. What if this was not a random happening, that he had contracted cancer, but he was part of a larger trial targeting the unluckiest of the human race? He knew this wasn't true, but being alone with his thoughts sometimes turned sort of devastating for him.

Rory turned Mary's letter over, his hand clammy now from clutching it after Alice had finished reading. Mary had jotted down a few more lines on the back. Ah, thought Rory, there it is. There was always a challenge, a task, that followed the memory that Mary dug up for him.

Rory, take Dex and Alice to the fair. Show them a beautiful night under the stars. Let them see you have fun, because you did, Rory. You used to know how to have fun. I want you to experience that same feeling again, and I want you to give Dex and Alice a good time.

Conquer your fear of the ferris wheel. I know it's scary. But so is dying. Oh, and I know you tried not to let me see how scared you were when we were at the top. But it's hard not to notice someone shaking so hard they might piss themselves. Ha ha, just my little joke. Anyway, do this for me, and I'll love you forever. Not that I don't already.

   Love always,
   Mary

"The York Fair!" Alice's voice startled Rory. He hadn't read the letter aloud, but Alice's curious nose was buried in the letter the entire time. "I love the fair, I'm sure they have one soon! And even if not, there's got to be one going on somewhere, it's that time of year." "Seriously?" Rory was surprised. "After what just happened, you think going on a roller coaster is a good idea?"

"We don't have to do the super-fast ones, but the Wheel would be fun!" Alice was getting too excited for Rory's liking. "Plus it's so romantic. And no offense, Rory, but your whole predicament with being sick all the time has kind of put a damper on Dex's and my intimacy. So I'll take whatever I can get."

Rory was too close with Alice to take offense to anything that came out of her mouth, so the pang in his gut wasn't caused by her words. It was the prospect of getting on a five-hundred-foot rotating wheel with nothing but an adolescent employee with a controller in his favour. He looked back at what Mary had written in her letter. *I know it's scary. But so is dying.* Did that mean that when she took those final breaths, that she was more terrified? Did she know what was happening, and frightened because no one was there to go through it with her? Or was Mary merely referring to the abstract idea of dying in general? Knowing that your end was imminent. Because if that's what she meant, thought Rory, then forget about dying. That's life.

Just then, Dex came home. He ran into Rory's room. As soon as he entered, Rory could tell he had rushed the whole way. His usually pale cheeks were flushed bright red, and his hair was mopped with sweat. Contrary to Rory's build, Dex was in much better shape, so Rory knew Dex had just been through a lot if he was this out of breath.

"Here," was all Dex could manage, as he handed the prescription to Alice, who administered the correct dose of medication to Rory. Dex, meanwhile, doubled over, putting his hands on his knees and concentrating on his respirations.

Rory took the medicine that Alice handed to him, gulping it down with a swig of water. He knew he wouldn't feel better immediately, but in five to ten minutes he would disappear into oblivion. As the room around him gradually grew more and more blurry, he thought of something that Mary had once said.

It's not what you're dealt but how you deal with it.

She was always spitting out rubbish like that, thought Rory, but she had a point. He was dealt some pretty unfortunate, cancerous cards. Dex had been dealt some pretty fortunate cards. Scholarships. High marks on all of his examinations. A position at his top choice hospital. Dex responded with gratitude and humility. Rory responded with bitterness and pessimism. What if their roles had been switched? What if Dex was the one swimming in the foggy room, bedridden, and Rory was the hero who had just run twenty blocks to get his brother his medicine? Would Alice still be by the bedside? Or would she be in the room at all? Circumstances, Rory decided, determined your fate. Not the other way around.

Ten

The sky was melting butter. At least, that's what Mary used to say when she and Rory would watch the sunset. It took a lot of convincing Dex, but finally, he agreed a week later that it would be safe to take Rory to the York Fair being held that month. After Dex and Alice returned from work one Friday afternoon, the three friends were off.

Rory's hands were clenched inside his pockets, and he was fighting back the urge to be sick. Ahead of him were Dex and Alice, both of whom were obviously feeling precisely the opposite. They were running toward the flashing lights and sirens of the festival rides. Rory trod slowly in their footsteps, having absolutely no interest in taking in his surroundings.

"Ooh!" cried Alice. "Dex, I want to ride the bumper cars! And the

Twister! You know, the one that spins round and round until you lose it! And-"

"What are you, five?" Rory interrupted.

Alice shot him a look of contempt from over her shoulder. "No, I'm fun. And excited! Come on, Rory!" She grabbed the crook of his elbow and linked her arm through it, still clutching Dex's hand. The three of them were inseparable once again.

"When was the last time you stepped outside and were able

to take a deep breath of fresh air?" Alice wanted to know.

The other day when I threw my guts up on the tube, Rory thought, but didn't answer.

"What do you want to do, Ror?" asked Dex.

"I dunno," Rory muttered.

"Well, what was Mary's favorite ride?"

"That would be the Big Wheel," Alice answered knowingly, looking for Dex's reaction. Rory was affronted that Alice was taking the piss.

"Oh, mate." Dex glanced at Rory with a look of pity. "That is really unfortunate for you."

"No, it's not!" Alice chirped. "Rory, this is perfect. Mary wanted you to experience life, right? Well, what's a better way to do that than to conquer your fears on the Big Wheel?"

"Er, a better way would be to go home, have a nice, cool glass of gin, and call it a night," Rory replied.

"Look, Ror," Dex said as Alice opened her mouth to form a retort, "say you don't want to do it, and we won't push it. But something tells me a little part of you wants to revisit the memory of that first, fantastically awkward ride with Mary."

Rory looked up at the Big Wheel straight ahead of them. It was as though it was looking down at him, taunting him with its size. He wasn't doing it for him. He wasn't even doing it for Mary. He was doing it because he wasn't going to let a bleeding observation wheel make him feel small.

Alice and Dex were the first to form the new line. They ran up to the ride holding hands. Rory wasn't too far behind them, but was stubborn enough to sulk while they enjoyed themselves.

"Two pounds per person," announced the carnival employee. Rory noticed that his eyebrows were so thick and close together that it gave him the appearance of having a unibrow. Dex handed him enough for himself and Alice, and the two of them got into the first compartment.

"Two pounds, mate," Unibrow told Rory as he stepped up. Rory paid, and since each compartment only held two people, he had to sit in the one behind the happy couple by himself. Once he was in, the giant wheel began to move, one space at a time. Slowly his car was making its way to the very top. He glanced down at the bottom; as people would exit their compartments, new passengers would enter them.

It wasn't until this moment that Rory had the sudden epiphany that life without him on Earth would go on. He was leaving early, and yet, the world would still spin. Alice and Dex would still wake up in the mornings, have breakfast together, and go to work. Even though Rory's world stopped when Mary died, that didn't mean anyone's world would stop when he died.

Surprisingly enough, this didn't depress Rory at all. In fact, he felt an overwhelming sense of comfort as his car went higher and higher. Alice was right about one thing, the fresh air was much needed. His car finally made it to the very top. He glanced down at the compartment in front of him to see Dex and Alice kissing, not realizing that they had already passed the top spot of the Wheel. Rory smirked at the sight. He was actually beginning to enjoy himself, and didn't even mind being so high off of the ground. The further he was from the ground, the smaller the world seemed to him. That was, until he felt a jerk and heard the screech of the controls from three hundred feet below.

Rory's muscles tensed up immediately, knowing what was coming next.

"Sorry 'bout that, chaps," Unibrow's voice echoed over the microphone. "There seems to be a small technical problem.

Don't worry though, we're going to get the ride working again in a few minutes, just stay put. And please remember to keep your hands and feet in the compartment." Rory squeezed his eyes tight and tried to focus on his breathing. His chest tightened, and his heart felt like it was going to leap out. With each beat, he felt like his heart was being compressed, until Rory found himself gasping for air.

Dex and Alice turned around to face Rory, both of them sporting worried expressions.

"Rory," Dex shouted to him. "Mate, it's alright. It's really not that high, just stay put, alright?"

Rory opened his eyes, which were damp from squinting so hard. He couldn't explain why, but he started rocking back and forth in his compartment, which in turn caused the compartment to do the same. He began shaking his head and muttering, "No, no, no!"

"Rory," Dex repeated, "focus. It's alright."

"Hang on, Rory!" cried Alice. "Don't look down, alright?"

But it was too late. Rory had glanced down below and did not have the same feeling he did just minutes before. Instead of feeling like he was flying, he felt as though he was plummeting to the ground. Or at least his stomach was.

"Rory," Alice said, sounding almost annoyed, "I can't help you if you don't listen to me."

"You have to get over this fear," Dex yelled up to him. "You're not going to fall out or anything. Just stay calm."

"No, it's not that," said Rory. "I'm losing it. I'm going to be sick. I need to get out."

"They've nearly fixed it, Rory," Dex looked down at the engineers repairing the ride. He had no idea if they were almost finished or not, but he knew that if his brother was panicked enough he might just try to jump out. "Just hold tight, do you think you can do that?"

Rory shook his head. "I don't know, I don't feel well. I—-I don't know. I think I'm having a heart attack. Dex, please get them to hurry up."

Dex shouted down to the engineers, "Oi! Excuse me! Do we have an ETA on this thing?"

"We're working on it, have some patience, will you?" One of the workers shot back angrily.

Dex turned back to assess Rory but found him tapping his knee restlessly. Rory tried to stand up, causing his compartment to shake wildly. He steadied himself by holding out his arms as though on a tightrope.

Alice screamed. Dex stood up in unison with his brother. "Rory, don't!"

But their shouts were in vain. Rory had lost all sense of himself. He didn't know what to do, but he knew he couldn't stay in the compartment. "Dex, please, just…I don't know what to do – I need to get out—-Dex I NEED TO GET OUT!"

Alice was crying. "Rory, stop being an idiot and sit down!"

"I can't!" Why didn't she understand? Why didn't any of them understand that he couldn't be where he was anymore? He needed out.

"Oi!" yelled one of the already flustered engineers from below. "You at the top! Sit down!"

But neither brother responded. Dex reached out his right hand to Rory, steadying himself with his left one. Alice clutched Dex's waist with both her hands, keeping him balanced.

"Okay, Ror," he said. "It's alright. I've got you, look. Just look at me. You don't need out. You're already free." Dex didn't know exactly what the string of words was coming out of his

127

mouth, but he didn't have time to think about what he was saying. He was desperate to save his brother, even though an inkling on the back burner of his mind reminded him that this was inevitably an impossible task.

"Dex," Rory wept. "I can't. I don't know what to do." His eyes were heavy and sad.

"Well, sitting down would be a start!" cried Alice.

Rory didn't listen. He attempted to put a foot over the railing. His body seemed to be acting without consent from his brain. The part of his mind that should be telling him, Get a grip! You're going to kill yourself! was apparently comatose. His compartment swung forward, tilting Rory toward Dex. He grasped the railing for support, one leg still over the rail, his body contorted in an awkward pose.

"Rory," choked Dex. "I'm not going to be able to catch you if you jump. It's too far. So get back in your compartment and sit down. You will most certainly die if you don't."

"No, I won't," Rory shook his head. He looked at his brother, his eyes boring into Dex's. "You'll catch me. You're my big brother.

That's your job, isn't it?"

Just then, every passenger on the Wheel felt a jolt as it began to rotate again. Rory's compartment swung backward, forcing Rory to tumble into it. Alice let out an ear-piercing shriek.

"Rory!" Dex called out.

Rory grasped the railing once more and hoisted himself into his seat, revealing that he was, in fact, unharmed. He clutched the rail for support for the remainder of the ride, unable to keep his entire body from violently shaking. Finally, the Wheel stopped to let Dex and Alice off, and then Rory. The couple waited just beyond the exit gate for him, but Rory darted past them once he got off.

"I should have the bloody police called on you!" Unibrow shouted out as Rory ran past.

"Rory, what the hell were you thinking?" Dex yelled angrily. But Rory didn't stop. He finally reached a rubbish bin, bent over, and retched. Dex and Alice stopped in their tracks, watching him get sick.

They slowly approached him from behind, careful not to startle him. Dex gently rubbed Rory's upper back while he vomited. He remembered his mother doing the same to himself when they were younger. When Rory had expelled what felt like every ounce of sustenance he had in him, he looked up at their two pitifully concerned faces.

Rory wiped the corner of his mouth with his sleeve. "I'm sorry," he said dully. "I'm sorry I scared you." Neither of them said anything, they simply stared at him. "I must have had a panic attack or something. I dunno." He hung his head. The silence was deafening to him. He didn't know if they were devastated, angry, or simply lost for words. He looked around, and a small tent with a sign of a crystal ball caught his eye. It was the same tent set up for the psychic Mary had gone to all those years ago.

"No..." he muttered to himself. He had wondered for years what Mary could have possibly talked about with the psychic that made her react the way she had. It wasn't anything that should have caught anyone off guard, but Rory wasn't anyone. He had brought up the night only a few times since then and finally stopped after Mary got sincerely frustrated at him. He was only joking. She clearly was not.

Without a word to his companions, Rory set off toward the tent.

"Rory?" Alice called after him. "Where are you going?"

Rory didn't stop. If it was the same sign as ten years ago, maybe, just maybe it was the same woman, Rory thought. He needed to know what made Mary so…impressed by what the nutter had said. He whipped open the tent to find an elderly Indian woman smoking a long cigarette, legs propped up and reading a book. She looked over as Rory came in, and quickly sat up straight.

"That'll be ten pounds, sonny." Her voice was raspy and indelicate.

"Ten?" Rory said incredulously, but he dished out the money anyway and slammed it on the table. He wanted answers. "What's gotten you all uptight over there?" the old lady wanted to know.

"You're a psychic, shouldn't you be able to read my mind or something?" Rory said dully.

The woman smiled. "You think it's a load of rubbish, don't you? Well, let me tell you something. If you thought all of this," she gestured around her to her crystal ball and cards lying on the table, "was nonsense, you wouldn't be in here handing over ten pounds. Eh?"

"I'm not here for me," Rory said quickly. He wanted to get out of there as soon as possible. The stench of the incense was making his eyes and nose burn. "About ten years ago I came here with my girlfriend. She had cancer at the time. Now, I know it was a long time ago, but if you could remember who I was talking about, that'd be great."

The woman stared at him for a moment. "Why don't you take a seat and let me take a look at your hands? I feel I need to sense your aura before we get started."

"No, I don't want you to feel my aura, I don't want you to look in your crystal ball, I already know my future. I just need you to remember this girl. She was the most beautiful girl you've ever met. She wore bright, floral patterns and had short brown hair. She came out of your tent and had this expression on her face that…I don't know. I knew she had found something out that stayed with her, and she never told me what that was. I need you to tell me."

"Darling, I see about fifty people every night. I'm sorry, but I don't think I'm going to remember some teenage girl from ten years ago. I just had about ten adolescents come through here asking me if they were ever going to find love."

Rory shook his head. "She wouldn't have asked you something so trivial. It would have been deep, something special. Like her."

The woman stared at him for a moment, realizing that he was not going to let this go. Finally, she tilted her head back and clasped her hands across her abdomen. She took a few deep breaths and remained in this position for what Rory estimated to be about ten minutes. He was worried she was going to make him pay another ten quid. But finally, she opened her eyes, an enigmatic expression on her face.

"Her name was Mary," she stated.

"Yes," said Rory. He had purposefully hadn't told the mysterious woman Mary's name so that he would know she wasn't bull-shitting him.

"Oh, I remember Mary," the woman smiled. "She passed away a couple of months ago, didn't she?"

"Yes," Rory replied cautiously. "Don't try telling me you can read my mind."

"I wasn't going to," the woman said, almost annoyed. "I remember seeing it in the obituaries. I didn't make the connection then, but it makes sense now."

"So you remember her, then," Rory said hopefully.

"Oh, yes," the woman said sincerely. "So what did she ask you?"

The old woman studied the young man sitting in front of her. He was on the edge of his seat, waiting for an answer even if it might destroy him. He was waiting for the hope that she could not give him.

"What did you say your name was, dear?" she asked. "I didn't. It's Rory."

"Well, Rory, when your lovely Mary came to me, I told her to ask me anything she wanted to. She didn't ask me anything, though, except if I believed in God. And if I didn't believe in God, did I believe in miracles?"

Rory's eyes bore into her own, intimidating her. She didn't know if she should go on, but she continued anyway.

"I didn't know she was ill, at the time, or else I would have guessed she was wondering about her own fate. I also thought that maybe she was one of those people who tries to condemn what I do as witchcraft. She didn't seem that way, however. I could tell she was a religious one, that girl. But I could also tell that she had a sort of innocence about her…a naivety, if you will. I didn't need to read her aura to figure that one out. I think she just truly wanted to know if I believed in something spiritual. I wanted to bite her head off, honestly, but she was so sad-looking. And she had paid me for my time." Rory simply stared at her.

"Look, Rory," she continued. "Your girlfriend was a scared little girl at the time, looking for answers in places she shouldn't have been looking. Someone like her should not have come to me. I couldn't give her what she wanted, and I'm afraid I disappointed her."

Rory didn't say anything. The fumes from the incense were making his eyes water now, at least, that's what he hoped the woman thought. He was no longer looking at her, but looking at the deck of cards from which so many sought their fate. Mary always claimed to be completely faithful to God, but even she must have doubted time and again. She would have gone looking for answers in the wrong places and only been left with disillusionment. It explained her solemnness upon leaving the tent all those years ago, and why she clung so desperately to her faith from then on.

Rory had to get out of the tent. This place was toxic to him. He turned on his heel and, without a word, left the tent, taking the fresh air into his lungs in great gulps. Alice and Dex were standing, arms folded, waiting for him just as he had done for Mary. He rejoined them, and they left the carnival. He never learned the old woman's name.

Eleven

It was Alice's laugh that woke Rory with a start. He couldn't fathom how long it had been since he heard her laugh like that. Rory wondered how long it had been since he heard Mary laugh. It was long before she died, he knew that much. Dex didn't know how lucky he was, thought Rory. He needs to hang on to that sound. You never know when you're going to forget it.

Rory followed the sound of laughter, and it led him into the kitchen. Alice and Dex were sitting at the table, sipping tea. They were having an obviously amusing conversation, but Rory had no interest in what it was about. He had one thought on his mind, the same thought that had haunted him since the festival.

Rory cleared his throat, and Dex looked up at him.

"Oh hey there, Ror," he said. "I was just about to cook up some breakfast, what'll you have?"

"I want to go and see Mary today," Rory said, ignoring the question.

Alice and Dex paused. Alice's open smile slowly faltered into a grimace.

"I mean," Rory continued, "I want to visit her grave. In York. I should have gone while we were there for the festival, but I got scared.

It's…it's something I need to do."

Alice and Dex looked at each other. "Well, I mean, if that's what you need to do, then I suppose that's alright," Dex replied.

"It's just…" Rory didn't quite know how to ask for what he wanted without feeling like he had lost his independence completely. "I would really like it if you two would go with me." He looked down as he said it, never having been more interested in the polka-dot pattern of his socks.

Dex and Alice exchanged a look of compressed excitement.

"Of course we'll come with you, Rory," Dex finally said, controlling his composure.

"Great, let me just go and grab a couple of things." Rory hastily retreated to his room and shut the door. Alice let out a quiet squeal.

"Eee! He's voluntarily hanging out with us! And it was his idea!

Not ours, not Mary's, no one's!"

"He's just asked us to visit his dead wife's grave with him," Dex replied, amused. "I don't think that necessarily counts as him wanting to hang out with us."

"Hey, I'll take what I can get."

Within one hour the trio was on a train to York. Dex looked over at his brother as the train lurched forward, to see Rory staring rather intently out the opposite window. He was clutching a handful of envelopes so tightly that his knuckles had turned white. Dex had known better than to ask why Rory had them when he knew the answer was as obvious as it seemed.

"Alright, mate?" Dex prompted.

Rory didn't respond. He was still staring out the window, his lips slightly parted as he inhaled and exhaled. Alice nudged him lightly in his ribs.

"Hm?" Rory looked over at her.

"You okay?" Dex repeated.

"Yeah," Rory replied. "Just nerves."

"'Bout what?" Alice wanted to know.

Rory avoided her gaze. "I haven't exactly kept up with Mary's parents like I told them I would."

"Do you ever phone them up?" Dex asked.

After an uncomfortable silence, "No."

"Send them an e-mail?" Alice prodded.

Rory glared at her. "I don't even own a computer, Al."

Alice and Dex exchanged exasperated looks. The train continued on, occasionally stopping at various locations. The three of them sat mostly in silence for the remainder of the two-hour ride. Finally, the train halted at their stop, where they got off and went up the stairs. All three of them were forced to squint from the burning sun that greeted them as they emerged from the train.

Dex and Alice followed Rory's stride as he took off down Prince's Way. They walked for several miles until they reached the Abels' front door.

"Here we are," said Rory. After a moment of hesitation, he rapped three times on the door. Almost immediately, it swung open to reveal Mrs. Abel, wearing an apron and her hair tied back in a loose bun.

"Rory!" she cried. The surprised expression on her face harbored no resentment, and her eyes grew wide as she looked just past Rory. "Dex, Alice — darlings, what are you doing here?" Before any of them could answer, she beckoned them inside. "Here, here, come along." She shouted over her shoulder, "Mark, Rory is here!"

The three of them followed Mrs. Abel into the tiny kitchen

just beyond the entrance. The same kitchen Rory had not set foot in since the funeral. The scene displayed Mr. Abel slouching at the table cradling a full cup of tea, with considerably less hair than when Rory had last seen him.

"I've just made tea," Mrs. Abel continued. I'll put some on for you three. Please, have a sit-down!" She gestured to the empty chairs at the table.

"Hello, Rory." Mr. Abel shook Rory's hand as he pulled up a chair to the table. Dex and Alice joined him.

"Hello," Rory replied.

"Well, what brings you to our neck of the woods, then?" After Mrs. Abel filled the kettle and switched it on, she sat down next to Alice. "We expected a bit more from you, Rory. I understand that it's hard, what with living in London now and everything. What an adventure that must be! What's it like?"

"Well," Rory began, "it's been—-"

"What is it, son?" Mr. Abel interrupted.

"Sorry?"

He stared at Rory, knowingly, almost as if he was studying him.

"There's something, isn't there? Something you're not telling us."

Rory shook his head, but the guilt was plastered across his face.

Mr. Abel nodded. "How long, then?"

Mrs. Abel gasped. "Oh, Rory…no. Dear God, no."

Rory looked Mr. Abel in the eye. "The doctor gave me about two months. Optimistically speaking, of course. That was er… five weeks ago, I think? So a few weeks then, I suppose…" His voice trailed off dully.

"You should have told us, dear," Mrs. Abel said tearfully. "We would have come up. But you know doctors, they're getting stuff wrong all the time."

"Idiots, they are," Mr. Abel said gruffly.

Alice and Dex exchanged a subtle look across the table. No one else noticed, as Mrs. Abel had just gotten up to pour the tea from the shrieking kettle.

Mr. Abel continued. "It's true, you know. They gave Mary, what, two years? And she didn't live past one. They haven't a sliver of brains in those inflated heads of theirs."

"Er, Dex is actually a doctor, Mr. Abel," Rory said, stifling a laugh.

"Yeah, but don't worry about it," Dex said quickly. "I'm well aware of my inflated head. It's why I've got this one around, to deflate it for me." He glanced at Alice.

Mr. Abel smiled. Mrs. Abel brought a serving tray with three steaming mugs and passed them around. "So what really brings you our way, Rory?"

"I've come to visit Mary," Rory replied. "I know I haven't yet, and I apologize for that." He averted their gaze as he pronounced this last part.

Mr. Abel nodded. "How have you been getting along, then? Without Mary?"

Rory paused. "She wrote to me."

"Sorry, love?" Mrs. Abel asked, confused.

"How else can I say it? She wrote me letters. She gave them to
Alice before she passed."

Mr. Abel took a deep breath, with the slightest of grins on his face. "She always did love writing. Adored it, she did. When I didn't see her nose buried in one of her travel books, she was surrounded by paper and pencils. She'd write poems, journals, short stories...you name it."

"You know, now that I think about it, I think I even kept some from when she was in primary school," Mrs. Abel added. "Always thought she'd make a living off it."

Mr. Abel shook his head. "She did it for the love of it. No deadlines. Only when inspiration hit. No keeping track of how much she wrote in a day or what time it was to write. Not like with everything else she had to be responsible for. Medicine... Doctor's appointments..."

Mrs. Abel turned to Rory. "So what sort of things did she write to you?"

"Well," Rory said hesitantly, "They've been pretty nostalgic for the most part. Although," he chuckled. "To be honest, she's persuaded me to do some pretty strange things."

"How do you mean?"

"Like, she told me I should steal a pregnancy test from Wilko. For a laugh. She thought I needed the adrenaline rush, or what have you."

"That's preposterous!" Mrs. Abel exclaimed.

"Right!" Alice laughed.

"Wait a moment." Mr. Abel got up from his chair and disappeared into the adjoining living room. After a moment he returned with a laptop computer. "I just saw this on the YouTube a while ago."

"It's just 'YouTube,' Mark," Mrs. Abel corrected her husband.

"What?"

"It's only YouTube, there's no 'The.'"

"That's what I said, isn't it?"

"Oh, never mind." Mrs. Abel was exasperated.

Mr. Abel began typing away. "Now, I know my eyesight has been failing me recently, but do tell me if I am mistaken in believing that this is you."

He turned the computer screen toward Rory, showing him a part of the video that Alice filmed of him running out of the store with the pregnancy test in his hand. The only part the camera got was the back of his head. In the background, Rory could hear the store clerk yelling at him and Alice.

"Our friends showed it to us the other day," Mr. Abel continued after the video had finished. "They said it was a virus!"

"They said it went viral, Mark," said Mrs. Abel, shaking her head.

"What's the difference?"

"Wait," Rory interrupted the couple. "How did this even get on the internet?"

"Someone must have filmed you and put it up for a laugh, dear," Mrs. Abel replied.

Rory slowly turned to look at Alice.

"Yeah," Alice said, looking every which way besides at Rory. "Rude of them…" Dex was failing in an attempt to hide his laughter in the palm of his hand.

"That was you, then, Rory?" Mr. Abel asked incredulously. "You sounded like you were having a right time of yourself. Hell, it gave me a laugh. And mind you, it's been a while since this house has heard one."

Rory's smile slowly withered away, and he looked at Mr. Abel intently, who in turn was staring at the table. It had only been a little over a month, but that was all it had taken to rob this man of what little light he had left in him. Rory had to live with this debilitating illness, but Mary's parents had to figure out how to live. He racked his brain for the right thing to say to this broken man. But alas, no words of comfort had ever worked on Rory.

They were less likely to work on

Mr. Abel. Finally, Rory said the only thing he thought would be helpful in the present situation.

"Let's watch it again."

Rory had convinced Dex and Alice to stop at the florist on the way to the cemetery. After several minutes of looking at the meager selection of flowers, Rory finally decided on a potted yellow sunflower.

It reminded him of a skirt Mary used to wear every first day of summer.

They continued from the florist on the walk to the gravesite. It wasn't a long walk from the Abels' house. Rory remembered the walk well…too well, from the procession only a few weeks prior.

They finally reached the top of the hill, where several head-stones sprinkled the earth. Rory clutched his plant tightly as they walked around looking for the one belonging to Mary. The tombstone had not been there the last time Rory was there, which was for the burial. It didn't take long to find it. It was the most decorated one by far. It was covered in fresh roses, pictures of her laughing with people Rory had never met, and stuffed animals.

"People must come here at least once a week," Dex observed.

"Those roses are definitely fresh," Alice agreed.

Rory couldn't put a name to what he was feeling. He stood in stunned silence, looking at the décor. Who had come to change the flowers so often? The most obvious guess was Mary's parents, but then who had taken the time to put the framed pictures and stuffed animals? Rory wondered how he could have been the most important part of her life when he had never been introduced to the parts that weren't centered on her illness.

Rory cocked his head toward his two companions. "Do you think you two could give me a moment? Just one moment of privacy, with

Mary?"

Dex clapped his brother on the shoulder. "Course."

Rory nodded and turned to the grave. Dex took Alice by the crook of her elbow, and she hesitated only briefly before allowing him to lead her down the hill. The two of them waited, watching Rory from a distance.

Rory stood awkwardly, looking down at the headstone before kneeling.

"I brought you a plant." He snickered, looking around at the other gifts that had been placed carefully by her stone. "Although, compared with this lot, I see I may have slacked off a bit on the gift-bearing aspect of the visit."

He shook his head. He couldn't form the words he had been longing to say since they last parted. "It's silly," he finally spoke. "Talking to you like you can hear me." He looked up at the headstone, reading for the first time what had been engraved:

Mary Amelia Abel
1990-2014
Loving daughter and friend

Rory recalled how Mary refused to have "Rest in Peace" etched onto her tombstone. "I will be at peace, but I won't be resting," she had told Rory. "I will be dancing among galaxies, and singing in the heavens."

Was the description on the stone the only summary of Mary's life that would ever exist? As far as Rory was concerned, Mary deserved to have an entire series of biographies written about her. But maybe she was only that interesting to him.

"I've been reading your letters," Rory said finally. "But you know that. You've got me doing some weird stuff, Mare. Making me look like a fool. But I get it. I understand you now. I understand why you resented me. It should have been me, Mary. I should have...snuffed it first. You should be the one jumping off trains, seeing the world, doing whatever else it is you have in store for me. What if I hadn't tried to off myself, hm? Would Alice still have given me your letters? Would you still have taught me to live if I hadn't so badly wished to die?"

Words were now coming out like vomit. As much as he wanted to, Rory couldn't help himself.

"I'm sorry, Mary. I'm not the same bitter man anymore, I truly am not. I just..." He now could say out loud what had plagued his conscience for months now. "I didn't come here to yell at you, Mare. I don't know why I brought that up. It's just, these things you're having me do...Did you mean to stir up so many memories? Because you see, Mary, although there is so much beauty in nostalgia, there is also the pain of the fact that those events can never be recreated with the people that matter. And every time those things are brought back to life, it's like a piece of you is being brought back to life as well. But then, in a blink of an eye, the memory is over, and it's as though you've died all over again. How could you do that to me?"

These last words carried through the open, empty field. He half expected to hear Mary's voice respond, or for one of the letters he was carrying with him to spontaneously open and have a clever response already written out. But none of this happened. So Rory continued.

"I know that you never intended to cause me pain, Mary. Just like I never intended to cause you pain, by keeping you hidden from the world you so longed to be a part of. I just…I need you to know that I never did it on purpose." His voice began to break, but he kept going.

"I only meant to keep you alive longer. I didn't want to lose you before I absolutely had to. I…" But he couldn't continue any further. His sobs racked his body, and he lurched forward, putting his hands on the green grass for support. He began to hyperventilate, and couldn't control his breathing. He suddenly felt two strong arms around his chest, and they gripped him tightly. Dex steadied him and held on to his brother until the sun began to set half an hour later. Finally, the two got up, brushed themselves off, and rejoined their companion at the bottom of the hill.

"How do you feel, Ror?" Alice finally spoke when they reached the cobblestone sidewalk.

"Like I should have visited long before now," Rory replied. It was getting dim outside, but he could still see the glow of Alice's face as she beamed at him.

"Well, maybe we can come back next weekend," Dex suggested.

"Make it a weekly occasion."

"Nah," said Rory. "I mean, thank you for the offer and everything, but you guys don't have to come with me. I'm fine making the trip on my own."

"We know," replied Alice. "We want to, though. You're not the only one who misses Mary."

Rory looked back at her and smiled, his silent acceptance. They continued retracing their steps until Rory suddenly stopped in his tracks. He backed up to a building they had just passed by, and he peered in the window.

"Oh, my god," Rory said in awe.

"What is it?" asked Dex, both he and Alice joining Rory at the window.

"This is where I used to have group therapy. This is where I met

Mary."

"We have to go in, then!" Alice exclaimed. "It's what, seven o' clock? They may be meeting today!" She reached for the door.

"Alice, no," Dex reached across to block her from turning the doorknob. "Don't force him to go in. It didn't work when Mum did it, it's not going to work now."

"No, I want to go," Rory said softly.

"What?" Dex looked at him incredulously.

"I want to go in," Rory said simply. And with that he swung the door to the community center open, and entered the building. Alice looked at Dex with her eyebrows raised, as if to say: I told you so. She followed Rory inside, and Dex trailed after her.

Rory made his way down the hallway to the room at the end. When he went inside, the room was buzzing with mindless chatter, little groups of people all mingling with one another. Some were bald, some in wheelchairs, and some looked as though they had never had so much as a cold before in their lives. But Rory knew better than to assume they were healthy. Some of the deadliest killers were the silent ones.

Rory instantly spotted who the group leader was, even though he had never seen him before in his life. He was a middle-aged man who clapped his hands together almost immediately after the trio entered. He asked everyone to take a seat in the circumscribed pattern of chairs in the middle of the room. Rory led his friends to find seats in the circle. Before he could say

145

anything, the leader recognized them as new faces.

"It looks like we have some new friends joining us today," he said. "Welcome, I'm Tom."

"Cheers, mate, I'm Rory."

"Hi Rory," a chorus of monotonous voices responded.

"And, er, I was diagnosed with osteosarcoma when I was fourteen and, long story short, it has now set up camp in my lungs."

The group stared at him, giving him their full attention. Facial expressions varied from sorrow to fear.

Rory continued, "I grew up here in York, a little house not too far from here. I actually came to this group as a kid after I was first diagnosed. And believe me, I know what some of you are thinking. Maybe your parents are making you come here for social support, or just some exposure to a social life in general. I dunno. But I hated

Group. Absolutely hated it."

Tom just stared at him. Obviously, whatever sort of wise advice from a seasoned alumn he expected was not what he was going to get.

"But it's important," Rory went on. "This is a great place for people like you guys. People like us, I suppose. It's where I met the love of my life, in fact. Her name was Mary. She enjoyed these meetings. They were really important to her. And it truly is a good place for friendship and support."

"Where is Mary now?" a rather mousy-haired boy asked.

Rory paused. "She passed away a couple of months ago."

"We're sorry to hear that, Rory," Tom sympathized.

"Thank you," Rory replied. "You know, after she passed, I sort of forgot everything I learned here. About how there is always at least one person who will miss you when you're gone. About how there is another person, always, out there who would give their life for yours.

Who loves you more than you love them. I forgot about all of that. Because to me, Mary was all of that in one. And I confess I fell into this sinkhole of self-pity. I was so lost. But in getting lost, I found hope in the two people who never failed me. Even though I have failed them…more times than I can count." Rory looked at Dex and Alice, who returned his gaze.

"They must be very good friends," Tom said.

Rory continued to look at Dex and Alice. He nodded. "They're

the best."

Twelve

ummer, 2006

The music was making the tiny, two-story house shake. Rory would have never known that his abode would accommodate one hundred guests (albeit quite uncomfortably) if Dex hadn't decided to throw a party on the weekend his parents had decided to go on holiday, just the two of them. Looking around the house, Rory could only identify two people he recognized other than his brother: Alice and Mary.

The three of them had never been partying together, and Mary wasn't aware of the partying Rory and Alice used to do on their own, usually involving alcohol and some mild recreational drug of their choice. That was a long time ago for both of them, but some of Alice's drinking habits died hard. Rory and Mary had already been entertained by Alice's striptease on the coffee table, which was interrupted only when Mary ushered her off in an effort to prevent her from further humiliation.

"Come along, Al," Mary said.

"You're not my mum, Maryyyy." She drew out the last syllable for several seconds. Mary looked amused.

"Alice, you really need to sort yourself out," Rory warned, but he too was smiling.

"Hold up," Alice said, suddenly thrusting up her palm in his face. "I need to go see someone about…something." She took off toward a couple talking in the kitchen.

As she approached the fridge to get another can of beer, she began eavesdropping on a conversation between Dex and a girl she assumed to be from his university. The girl was intoxicated and absentmindedly stroking Dex's arm, which filled out the sleeve of his sweater perfectly.

"It must be so hard, Dex, to be away from your brother while you're at uni," she was saying.

"Er, it's alright. I see him on weekends," Dex replied.

"I still can't believe the things he has to deal with…the things *you* have to deal with. Is that what got you interested in medicine?"

"Yeah, I suppose it is. I never really thought about it."

"I have a sister," the girl continued.

Stop being an idiot, Alice thought. "And I can't imagine what I would do if I lost her."

"Excuse me," Dex said, and he walked past the girl and out of the kitchen.

"Can you believe that about Dex's brother?" the girl asked Alice, who had closed the refrigerator door and opened her can.

"No, I can't," Alice said, after taking a large gulp. "I can't believe people like Rory and Mary have to die early while bimbos like you get to live long and ignorantly blissful lives." She left the kitchen, leaving the girl sporting a vacantly shocked expression on her face.

Alice couldn't see straight. She found Rory across the room and stumbled toward him, attempting (and failing) to keep him in her focus. She reached out to him with the hand that wasn't clutching her can of beer. He grabbed her and steadied her.

"Whoa, Al, how much have you had?"

"Just enough," Alice slurred.

"Just enough for what?"

"To finally express my undying love for your brother. With no fear of reper...repercussions," Alice hiccupped.

"Alice, I hate to break it to you, but Dex already knows," Rory laughed.

"No, he doesn't!" Alice whined.

"Actually Al," Mary appeared behind her holding a coke. "I'm afraid this is one time our Rory is right about something, and you're wrong."

Alice began to cry. "But I've been so careful not to let anything slip! Just because I'm a little tipsy—-"

Rory laughed. "Alice, Dex didn't discover you fancy him tonight."

"When, then?"

"Probably since the beginning of our friendship," Rory replied.

"You're not exactly the most inconspicuous."

Alice wailed. "But if he hasn't made a move on me, then that means he doesn't fancy me!"

Rory shrugged. "I'm sorry, Alice, I don't know what to tell you.

Except that you're really putting a damper on this party."

Alice plopped down in a chair in the living room. "He doesn't talk to me. He hardly even looks at me anymore. Am I really that ugly?" She looked up at Rory and Mary, mascara cascading down her face.

"Of course you're not, Alice," Mary sat down next to her and put an arm around her shoulders. "But you are pissed. And you probably need a lie-down."

Alice groaned as Mary took her by the hand to Rory's room.

There she made sure Alice was comfortable in Rory's bed before turning out the light and closing the door.

Mary made her way back down the stairs to find Rory standing by himself, still in the living room.

"Are you having a good time?" she had to yell in order to be heard over the music blaring, some sort of rap that one of Dex's mates had chosen.

"Not really," Rory shouted. They both laughed. "Why did Dex think this was a good idea?"

"You think your parents will mind?" Mary asked.

"No, because it's Dex. If it were me, it'd be another story."
"Why is that?"

"Because they think I'm incapable of doing anything without accidentally putting myself in the warm, open arms of death," Rory replied. He took a sip from the bottle he was holding.

Alice woke up from dozing off and on. She was beginning to sober up and needed some water. Her mouth felt like a cotton ball and she was sure that she either needed to vomit or eat a ham and cheese toastie. She stumbled out of Rory's bed and into the toilet which connected his room to Dex's. She turned the knob and entered.

But someone was already leaning over the sink.

Dex looked up at the mirror above the sink, startled. He saw Alice in the reflection, and Alice saw him. She saw the red in his eyes and the tears that were streaming down his cheeks. His usually slicked-back hair was a mess, and his lips were the shiny purple color they turn when you breathe in and out aggressively for an extended period of time. He inhaled deeply and turned around to face Alice, wiping his nose with his sleeve.

"I'm—-I'm sorry," Alice said, unsure what exactly she was apologizing for. She quickly turned on her heel and ran down the stairs.

Rory and Mary took Rory's bed while Alice slept on the couch, as was the three friends' usual routine now that Mary was in the picture. No more kipping at the end of the bed for Alice, not that Mary would mind. But Alice, even though she could be immature at times, understood boundaries.

Alice made herself breakfast the next morning; everyone from the night before had left around four in the morning. Therefore, coffee was the first thing she grabbed when she entered the kitchen. She didn't hear Dex come in behind her.

"Hey, Alice," Dex rasped. His voice was hoarse from screaming along to rap lyrics from the night before.

"Hiya," Alice turned around to face him. "Coffee?"

"Please." He began helping her put the kettle on for hot water.

"Listen, Alice, I wanted to talk to you about what you saw last night." "What do you mean?"

"You don't have to play stupid, Al. You walked in on me upset. And I know you were drinking, but I have enough experience with girls who are pissed to know you definitely remember."

Alice avoided eye contact with him and got down the instant coffee from the cupboard.

"I just wanted to explain that I was pissed as well, and what you saw was the result of partying too hard and drinking too much. This girl had asked me about Rory's illness, and that along with everything else just set me off. Honest, that's all. I'm not usually like that. It was just I had a lot to drink," he repeated.

"That's alright," Alice said, finally looking at him.

"Good," Dex said.

"But even if it wasn't because you were pissed, that'd be alright too," she said.

Dex stared at her. "What do you mean?"

"I mean, I think that you really care about Rory. And you're scared for him. I'm scared for him too, Dex. I worry about him all the time. But I worry about you as well. Because…because I love you."

"Yeah, I love you too," Dex said, patting her on the shoulder.

"No," Alice shrugged him off. "I mean, I really, really love you." There it was. She had said it. And then she threw up all over Dex's feet.

"Oh my god, I'm so sorry!" she choked.

"Er…Don't worry about it," Dex said, reaching for a towel. He ran it under tap water and began cleaning his feet, then the floor.

"No, Dex, oh my god, I can't believe this is happening," Alice covered her face with her hands and slid down onto the cold, tiled floor.

Dex finished cleaning up the vomit and threw the rag in the sink. "Look, Al, seriously, I've cleaned up after girls who were way more hungover than you. Really, you're alright."

"Exactly," Alice uncovered her face. "You've dealt with so many other girls. So many who you probably would rather be standing in your kitchen right now than me."

"Alice, I can honestly say that I'd rather have you puking in my kitchen than have any other girl standing here."

Alice eyed him. "Thanks?"

Dex laughed. "It's alright."

Alice shook her head. "I can't believe I told you I love you. You don't love me…that's alright. I get it. I am your little brother's best friend. How could you like someone like me?" She ran her fingers through her long, tangled hair.

Dex didn't say anything for a moment. He had never seen Alice like this before. So vulnerable, so unsure of herself. He bent down and put his hand on her knee.

"Alice, I wish that I could tell you, in complete honesty, what I have been thinking for the past four years," he said earnestly.

"That you love me, too?" Alice whispered breathlessly, her heart pounding. "Then why don't you just say it?"

Dex gestured at the towel covered in Alice's vomit that he had just thrown into the sink.

"I actually thought I just did."

Present Day

It had been five days since Rory read one of Mary's letters. He was doing the best he could to ration them.

One Sunday he found himself wandering into his bedroom and reaching in his bedside table drawer to pull out the package. He took out the next individually wrapped letter in line and sat on his bed to indulge.

Hi Rory,

It seems the days I have left are dwindling on me. It's getting more and more challenging to write these letters because you won't leave me alone for five minutes by myself! I don't have the nerve to tell you I'm bothered though; you're just too sweet and sad. As the days get shorter and shorter, I'm finding it more difficult to remember a time when I felt hopeful. And it's taken a lot of racking my brain to find a specific memory. But I finally got one.

Summer, 2006

Rory and Mary were walking along the nearly empty street parallel to her house. Mary hadn't spoken to him much that night, but Rory hardly noticed. He was too busy sharing, quite animatedly, the news of Dex and Alice's blossoming relationship.

"I mean, it's about time they got together," he was saying. "Alice would always seek me out after school asking me about Dex, and Dex was always asking me about her. Since Alice just turned eighteen, he asked her out! I honestly haven't seen Dex this happy in years. Usually he's stressed out studying for exams. I suppose it'll be hard for them come September when he goes back to uni. I don't even know where Alice is going. She refuses to talk about it since we left school. I think she's in denial that we are actually a part of the real world now. I dunno, though. I think they are two of the good ones. I can see Dex committing, but I dunno about Alice. She's a bit of a free spirit if you ask me. You alright?" He finally realized that Mary was silently weeping. Pain was Rory's first assumption. Headache...nausea...tumor. He stopped Mary in her tracks and turned her toward him. "Mary," he said quietly.

She turned her face up to his. "What? Oh, I'm sorry, Rory. I'm...Actually, no. I'm not alright."

Rory's heart skipped a beat. He knew it. There was new tumor growth. She was about to deliver her death sentence to him. His chest constricted and forgot for a moment how to breathe properly.

"You're ill," Rory said.

"No," Mary shook her head. "I mean, not more so than usual... I'm moving."

"Come again?"

155

"I'm moving, Rory." Mary looked away, unable to stop the stream of tears that picked up its pace. "My uncle got a promotion at a research hospital in Wales. He's arranged it so I could get a spot in this trial he and his colleague are conducting. I dunno much about it, but it's pretty much a no-brainer. I mean, my parents think it's the best shot I've got. They're not thrilled about me moving away, but they know I'll be in the capable hands of my uncle, and he's a doctor and everything. They have to stay here with the shop. And I'm eighteen now and all. They're insisting I move to Wales."

Rory was speechless. He didn't know what he was supposed to say. "Whoa," was all he could manage.

"You could come too," Mary said, her voice small. "What?"

"I talked to my uncle," she continued hesitantly. "You could still get your treatment, and if a trial were to come up, you could possibly get a spot as well. Rory, we could move away together and finally start our lives, just as we've always talked about!"

Rory was overwhelmed by the magnitude of what Mary was offering him. He would get a fresh start with the love of his life... but what about his family? And his friends—well, he thought, he supposed Mary was his only friend. Besides Alice. But Alice would have Dex. He would probably see less of Alice now anyway since she would surely spend all her free time with Dex...

And he was eighteen. Mary was right. They were adults now. They could make their own decisions. And they didn't exactly have plans on going to university, given the circumstances. Having cancer was a full-time job for both of them.

Mary waited patiently for Rory to respond. When he did, he took Mary by the hand.

"I don't know if I can do this, Mare. My mum needs me to

help out around the house, and my dad—-"

"This is the best thing for us, Rory," Mary said assertively. "For everyone. I...I can't move on my own. Yes, I will get the treatment I need, and it will quite possibly save my life. But my parents are staying here to run the bookshop. That place is their livelihood. They can't move with me. I need you." By now Mary's tears had transitioned from silent to loud, nearly unbearable sobs. Rory pulled her into his chest and held her there.

"Okay," he said.

Mary broke away from him to look at his face, seeing if he was serious. "Really?"

Rory nodded. "I go where you go, darling."

"But...I mean I thought you would need to talk to your parents first."

Rory shook his head. "No need. I already know what they would say. And it's not the answer we want to hear."

"This is crazy," Mary said, smiling. "We're actually moving to Wales. On our own! This is so adult of us!"

Rory tried to share the excitement, but one thought kept plaguing his mind. "I don't know how to tell them."

Mary took his hands in her own. "Write it all out in a letter."

"I'm not exactly a man with many words, Mary."

"It'll help," she replied. "I promise."

One week later, Mary found herself standing at the station, alone. It was ten fifty-three at night, and the train was leaving at eleven o'clock. She was becoming nervous. She had already texted Rory three times asking where he was. At ten fifty-six, she felt a hand tap her on the shoulder.

She spun around, exhaling in relief. Rory took her bags from her hands and swung them over his shoulder.

"I thought for a terrifying second you weren't going to make it," Mary confessed.

"I told you what my decision was. It's you."

"You never answered my text messages. What did your parents say?" Mary asked anxiously.

"Nothing," Rory replied.

"What?"

"I wrote them a letter, just like you suggested. And then I left it on the kitchen counter and snuck out the back door. They will see it in the morning."

"Rory," Mary was astonished. "You cannot just move out of the house you've been living in for eighteen years and not tell your parents!"

"Look, it's better this way. Believe me," Rory insisted.

"But what's going to happen when they wake up and find out you're gone, and all they have left is a note?"

Rory was annoyed that Mary was making such a massive deal about this. The sacrifice he was making was for her, and yet she was still pointing out everything wrong with the way he handled things.

"I'll tell you exactly what will happen," he said, looking her directly in the eye. "My mum will go downstairs tomorrow morning before the sun even comes up, to put on coffee for my dad before he wakes. She won't see the letter on the kitchen counter at first because of the clutter around it. When she reaches for the drawer to get a spoon out, she will notice the slip of paper by the words 'Mum and Dad.' She will unfold it curiously. As she begins to read about your uncle and the opportunity that awaits us in Wales, the look on her face will transform from curiosity to confusion, and finally to horror.

She'll cry out in shock, waking my dad. He will shuffle down the stairs in confusion, and my mum, lost for words, will simply hand him the letter. He then will read between the lines of how this is a good opportunity for the family financially. He will twist my words and believe that I am calling him a failure. Finally, they will read the address of your uncle's house, and how, if they ever decide to forgive me, they know where they can reach me. And lastly how I still, and always will, love them."

Mary was shocked. "And you're okay with all of that?"

"I'm here, aren't I?"

"Rory-"

"It's for the best," Rory interrupted her. "For all of us, I promise."

The train pulled up just then, at exactly eleven o'clock. By this time a few other passengers had crowded around the yellow boundary line. As soon as the doors slid open, Rory headed to the first two open seats. Mary followed slowly behind him, with a look of hesitation on her face. The train doors slid shut.

"Where is he?" Alice demanded, pushing through Dex before he could fully open the door. "Alice, wait—-" Dex's attempts to calm his girlfriend were in vain.

"Where is he?" Alice repeated, this time to Mr. and Mrs. Gallagher, who were sitting at the kitchen table. Sarah was clutching a piece of paper in her hands, trembling. Arthur's expression was stoic, and his posture was as stiff as a board.

"He's gone," Dex knifed through the silence. This sent Sarah into a flood of tears.

"What do you mean, gone?" Alice asked Dex while staring at

Sarah.

"He's gone to Wales, Alice, just like I told you over the phone. He left a letter explaining everything."

Sarah clutched the piece of paper even tighter to her chest.

"Wales?" Alice cried, nearly laughing. "What could there possibly be for him in Wales?"

"Everything, apparently, that is better than what he had here," Arthur's voice was quiet but gruff.

The four of them didn't say anything after that. Alice was furious. In her opinion, everything would be better off if Rory hadn't screwed everything up by going out with Mary in the first place. Mary messed up the chemistry the three friends had, and they were doing alright, thank-you-very-much, before she showed up.

"Well, we just have to go and get him," Alice finally offered.

"Alice, we can't," Dex shook his head at her as if it were so foolish of her to assume she was more important to him than the reason he left his entire family behind.

"He loves that girl too much to be apart from her," Sarah whispered.

"Even if he wanted to come back," Arthur spoke up, his voice no longer quiet and gruff, but fierce. "He will never be allowed under my roof again. No son of mine abandons his family after they gave him all they had to offer. Maybe it wasn't enough, but it was all we could do for the boy. We got him his treatments, yes? I took on extra shifts at the shop so Sarah could take off work to drive Rory to his appointments, didn't I, now? Well, if this is how he responds to a family's sacrifice, I won't have it."

With that, Arthur pushed back from the table and stormed out of the kitchen, leaving Sarah in tears and the two adolescents in shock.

Alice turned to Dex. "This is all my fault."

"How did you work that one out, Al?" Dex tested her.

"The other day, I told Rory…I told him that the puppy love he and Mary shared was just that — puppy love. I told him it wouldn't last."

"Alice."

"I know, I know. I shouldn't have said it, but we were all thinking it! You know we were! I told him that she was too strong in her faith in God to ever give it up for him, and that he was too stubborn to ever buy into what she believed. That was nearly a week ago. We haven't spoken since."

Dex shook his head. "Rory needs to be able to take control over the very few things he has control over. This is one of those things."

"Yes, but listen—-"

"No, Alice, you listen to me," Dex cut her off. "Rory has found someone that finally makes him happy. Someone who relates to both his trials and his victories. Neither one of us has the ability to do that, thank god."

"You can't give up on him, Dex!"

"I haven't Al, can't you see? I'm letting him go. Take a moment and think about why you care so much that he chose to move away with Mary. I think someone should give Rory up. And that person isn't me, it's you."

Alice turned swiftly on her heel and walked briskly out of the kitchen, letting a sob escape her. Dex heard the front door open and slam shut. When he followed the hostile exit, though, he found Alice sitting on his stoop, crying.

Dex sat down next to her and put an arm around her tightly.

Alice leaned her head on Dex's shoulder, fitting like two pieces of a puzzle that had finally formed together. Alice wiped her eyes with the sleeve of her jumper.

"Rory's going to die, isn't he?" she said quietly. "Rory's going to die, and the last thing that I would have said to him is that he made poor relationship decisions."

"Don't talk about my brother like that," Dex shook his head.

"We both know the seriousness of Rory's illness, Dex," Alice pulled away and looked into his eyes. "What if he doesn't follow his treatment? What if he gets worse and we never know because he won't contact us?"

Dex's eyes welled up at that, but he refused to let them spill over. He attempted to cover up this slip of vulnerability by looking away from Alice. She mistook this as a cue that she had said too much. She was pushing away the only person she had left, and she was damned if she would let that happen.

"Look," Alice wrapped her own arm around Dex. "I'm sorry.

Maybe the doctors will be really good in Wales, and Rory will be okay.

Maybe he and Mary will even stay together and get married."

Dex half-laughed at that. "I don't see Rory as the marrying type."

"I don't either, really," Alice agreed with a slight smile. "But maybe he'll surprise us all."

Dex turned to her. "I think he's already sufficiently surprised us all for a lifetime, don't you?"

Present Day

Rory continued reading Mary's letter:

It's no wonder they hated me. After stealing you away like that in the dead of night. Although, to be fair to myself, I didn't think about the conflict it would cause between you and your parents. But you gave me more hope than that treatment trial could have. So

162

please know that I have thought of this next task very consciously and carefully: You need to make amends with your mother. She was never angry at you, Rory. She loves you and always will. Your father loves you too, but he is a very stubborn man who is set in his ways. It is not fair for you to dream at this point that he may come to his senses before you leave this world. But your mother already has. She is just too afraid to do anything about it. Remember how I used to try to memorize Psalms and Proverbs? Proverbs 23:22 says, "Listen to your father who gave you life, and do not despise your mother when she is old."

I know that this may go in one ear and out the other, but what He is saying is that it pleases Him when we listen to our parents. They fail us because they are human, Rory. But the time will come when you have the opportunity to forgive them for this treacherous curse of humanity that plagues us all, even you. After the thievery and jumping off of trains you've done for my honour, this is by far the riskiest. The greatest amount is at stake here. I will write again soon.

Your Mary

When Rory finished reading the letter, he stood, frozen. His expression was molded into one of disgust. Slowly, as he replayed the words Mary wrote over and over in his head, his expression turned to anger. Without thinking twice, he crumpled up the letter in his hand and threw it against the wall. It hardly made a sound. He looked around the room for something that he could break. He snatched the lamp off his bedside table and smashed it into the wall, relishing in the crash. He yanked the sheets and pillows off his unmade bed and flung them across the room, grunting and heaving.

Alice rushed into the room when she heard the commotion.

Rory was pacing the floor, running his hands through his hair.

"What the hell happened in here?" Alice cried.

"What was she thinking?" Rory demanded. "What the hell was she thinking? And trying to use her religion to justify it. I can't see her!

I can't talk to her!"

"Who?" Alice wanted to know. "Rory, what's happened? Why are you so upset?"

But Rory ignored her questions. "Her letters were supposed to help me, yes? They were supposed to help with the healing process, with the moving on part, right? Because she left me behind. That's what I am. I'm a Left Behind. And someday you and Dex will be Left

Behinds too, but I wouldn't dare do to you two what she's doing to me.

She's gone mad if she thinks I'm going to speak to her."

"Speak to Mary?" Alice was thoroughly confused. Finally, Rory stopped pacing to look at her.

"My mother," he snarled.

"Oh." Suddenly Alice understood.

"Mary wants me to make amends with my mother. And it's not like you or Dex suggested it. It's…It's different because it's Mary asking. So naturally, I have to do it. God, I'm so angry at her!" Rory took a seat at the foot of the practically destroyed bed. Alice stared down at him.

"No, you're not," she said simply.

Rory rubbed his eyes and looked up at her. "And where do you get off trying to tell me how I feel?"

"Because you're just like Toby," Alice replied, as if it were the most obvious thing in the world.

"Who?"

"One of my students, Toby. He comes from a rubbish family and lives in a shabby part of London. He goes to sleep not knowing if he's in a safe place every night. When he's not hearing gunshots outside his window, his parents are shooting up with heroin down the hall. It isn't right. So he comes to school angry about every other morning. He'll take a toy from one of the other kids just to make them cry. He'll rip up whatever paper he's supposed to be working on. And he has the most advanced, vulgar vocabulary of any five-year-old I know. But I know he's not angry at the other kids, or the paper, or me. He is angry at his situation. And his utter lack of control over it. He feels helpless. You

feel helpless too, Rory."

"What do you do with him?"

Alice sat next to Rory at the foot of the bed. "I sit him down. Give him a blank piece of paper and tell him to draw all over it. Make it as messy as possible. Get his frustration out. Calm him down. But you don't need to calm down, Rory. You need to get angry. You need to get really, really angry. Because right now, you're frustrated at the wrong thing. You need to yell, and kick, and scream, and cry because that's the only way you're going to accept that you're actually angry at the situation. And the cancer. So say it."

"Say what?"

"That you hate cancer," Alice prompted.

"Whatever," Rory shrugged.

"Rory," Alice sighed. "Say it. Because you know you're not angry at Mary."

"If I were able to say it," said Rory, "wouldn't I be saying that I regret meeting Mary? That I regret the thing that ultimately brought me the most joy in my life?"

Alice shook her head. "Rory, don't you see? It's not an insult to

Mary's memory to hate the thing that killed her. Even if it is the thing that brought you together. It's also the thing that ripped you apart. So say it. Say it now."

"I hate it," Rory muttered, looking at his hands.

"Hate what?"

"The cancer."

"Shout it!" exclaimed Alice. "Come on, you were just chucking everything against the wall two minutes ago. Get livid again, Rory!"

"I hate cancer," Rory said, raising his voice slightly.

"Come on Rory," Alice urged him, "that's not how you really feel, is it? Tell me how you feel about cancer!"

"I HATE CANCER!" Rory exploded. "I loathe it! I...I despise it!

It's wrecked me. It kept me from having a life for ten years, dammit! And it took my Mary, my beautiful, sweet Mary—-" he dropped to the floor to pick up the letter he had crumpled up. He unfolded it, still speaking, "the Mary who planned my remaining days without her, making sure I held on to a piece of her. Oh, Mary," Rory began to cry. "Of course I'm not cross with you, or your letters. I hate this intruding, toxic poison that captured you and stole you from me." His arms began to shake, and he hugged the letter to his chest, sobbing. Alice looked at him, solemn.

"There it is, then," she said. Rory looked up at her, hiccupping. He walked toward her and gave all his weight over to her. Alice held him up as he wept, bearing all the weight she possibly could. She wondered, now that she had broken her friend, how she could possibly put him back together.

Thirteen

Winter, 2008

"You missed the turn, it was that split in the road back there."

Alice was parched. Dex was driving, and the five-hour long journey to Rory and Mary's home in Wales had placed them both in sour moods.

"You missed it on purpose," Alice muttered.

"Alice, don't start."

"You don't want to see them, fine," Alice retorted hotly. "But I am famished, and I need to use the loo, so if you could just give me an estimated time of arrival, that'd be lovely."

Dex made a U-turn without braking, causing Alice to lean suddenly and hit her head on the window.

Alice glanced at him out of the corner of her eyes and smirked. "If you seriously didn't want to come, then why did you agree to this bloody trip?"

"It wasn't my decision, if you can recall. I can't just not show up after my brother's announced that he's gone and got married without telling anyone. And I just as well can't not go when

I have an obnoxious girlfriend telling me every five minutes what a terrible brother I am if I don't."

Alice sat quietly for a moment. Suddenly, a small cottage at the end of a very long road came into view. Her heart began palpitating at twice its usual rate, and her palms suddenly became very clammy. "I can't believe it's been two years since we saw them," she breathed.

"Dex, I don't think I'd gone more than two days without seeing Rory since I met him, and now it's been two years…What do we even say to him?"

Dex pulled into the drive next to the cottage. "You've had five hours to consider that. Time's up, my love."

Dex got out of the driver's seat and came around to open Alice's door for her. Before they made their way up to the stoop, the door opened. A hairless twenty-year-old Rory stepped out, followed by a matching Mary. Neither of them was wearing anything to cover their bare heads, and their beams took over their entire faces. Mary was the first one to reach them.

"Come here, you!" She threw her arms around Dex's neck, while

Alice shuffled uncomfortably nearby. "And you!" Mary did the same to Alice, pulling the two of them into an awkward, three-man hug. Rory remained in the doorway.

"Come on in, you two probably would like to freshen up a bit, wouldn't you?" Rory invited them inside. "Can't say I've got used to the cold yet, so I daresay you two find it most displeasing."

While Mary led Dex and Alice into the one-bedroom abode, Alice mouthed to her boyfriend, "Daresay find it most displeasing?" This bald, proper-speaking Rory was the complete opposite of that who had left Alice and Dex behind in York.

Sure, he had lost his hair before, but he always wore his signature black wooly cap around Alice.

The cottage screamed Mary. First of all, there was colour everywhere. There were random pictures of puppies scattered along the walls (the couple didn't even own a pet), and in the kitchen there were vintage pots and pans; unusable, yet hanging for decoration.

"What do you think?" Mary wanted to know.

"It's kitschy," Alice commented.

"I like it," Dex said, observing the space.

"It's a bit small, only one bedroom, so the two of you will have to make do with the inflatable camping mattress," said Rory. "I hope you find it comfortable enough."

"You mean in case we decide we simply can't resist each other, and have to jump each other's bones?" Alice said, laughing, glancing at Mary out of the corner of her eye.

Rory laughed awkwardly, and Mary smiled politely.

"I think we'll be fine," Dex said. "Thank you so much for having us over, Mary," he added, graciously.

"You two must be really tired from your trip," Mary commented. "Would you like to retire to the kitchen for a cup of tea?"

Dex nodded, but Alice spoke before he could. "I actually don't feel much like retiring just now. I fancy a walk around the town. Rory, you must show me all of the sights!" The mockery in her voice was not inconspicuous.

Mary's smile faltered. "What you saw on your way up is about it. I'm rather tired, but if you three would like to venture out, be my guest."

Dex straightened up. "Actually, I'd love a drink, Mary, if your offer is still good."

"Brilliant!" Alice said. "You two stay here and chat, and Rory and I can take a stroll. We have a lot of catching up to do." Alice couldn't hide the resentment in her voice any more than she could conceal her own skin.

Rory looked at Mary, who nodded. "Yeah, I guess that'd be… good."

Neither of the two friends said anything for twelve minutes.

They had reached the end of the road before Rory spoke.

"Is this your twisted version of 'Say Uncle?'"

"Sorry?"

"You know, like when we were kids. And we'd hold each other's arms behind their backs and wouldn't stop until some-one said 'Uncle.'"

"When we were kids…" Alice scoffed.

"What is your problem, Alice?"

That was all it took. Those five, simple words. What was the problem? Alice couldn't bear to look at him. Fury boiled up inside of her like a fire on which someone poured alcohol. The flames licked up her spine, and her neck turned red hot.

"The problem," she began, "is that you took off in the dead of night without a word! Not one word! All we got was a letter. A bloody letter, Rory, and it wasn't even addressed to me. It was for your parents! I didn't get anything! That's what eight years of friendship meant to you?"

Tears stung in the corners of her eyes, but she refused to let them spill over.

Rory stared at her. Alice didn't know what she expected, but what came next was nothing near it.

"Are you joking, Alice?"

She was stunned. "What?"

"That was two years ago."

"Exactly!" cried Alice. "Two years of radio silence! Only bits and pieces of information about your life delivered through Dex!"

"Alice, you don't realize that I have grown up since then. I'm able to put the past behind me. But you, you're in there making sex jokes and making Mary feel uncomfortable on purpose! I'm married, Alice. And I'm sorry that bothers you so much, but you're just going to have to get over it."

Alice stopped walking. "Why would that bother me?" "Because I got married first," Rory said bluntly.

"Excuse me?"

"Oh, Alice, come on. I know that you've been waiting for years for Dex to propose. I also happen to know that he will do no such thing until he passes all of his exams and gets hired somewhere full time, so best of luck with that. You feel as though Mary and I are more relationally mature than you two, and that makes you jealous."

"Please," Alice said, exasperated. "The only reason you married that girl is to get into her knickers."

She regretted it as soon as she said it. Alice knew, deep down, that this wasn't true. Of course it wasn't true, but that didn't make her pain any less real.

"Is that what you think?" Rory asked her.

Alice was in no position to back down. "Well, you said yourself she never let you get anywhere below the belt. And she's really, like Christian, or whatever. Plus you two are no friends of time, so I just thought—-"

"Hold up." Rory put his hand up to stop Alice from ranting any further. "Yes, Mary is, as you so delicately put it, 'Christian or whatever.' And I respect Mary and her beliefs. But the decision to be married to someone goes so much deeper than wanting to have sex,

Alice."

Alice wasn't looking at him. She decided to stare intently at a bird approximately fifty feet away, instead. Rory continued speaking nonetheless.

"You carry so much pride on your shoulders, Al, that you are incapable of admitting that you're wrong even when you know you are." Rory's words were not dealt to her harshly, but rather gently, as if trying to soften a blow.

"I love Mary," he went on. "And she loves me. Yes, we saved the most intimate part of our relationship until we got married. It was a decision we made together. I know that you think she's trying to manipulate me with her beliefs, but that's not it at all. Mary believes in something bigger than any of us. Bigger than you, than Dex, than me, even bigger than herself. While I wouldn't admit this to her, I wished I had the balls to believe in something like that myself. But Mary is all I've got. And I just feel like if I'm following her, then maybe I'll find what I'm looking for. And if in the end she's right, then what have I lost, really?"

After a moment, Alice looked him in the eyes, almost golden in the sunlight. "You really have changed," she said.

"Is that really such a terrible thing?"

The two friends rejoined their partners an hour later, linked arm and arm. The familiarity of this gesture put Alice at ease, and when she reached the cottage, she kissed her friend on the cheek.

"I will always support you, no matter your choices," she whispered so only he could hear, for Dex and Mary were still conversing in the kitchen.

"I would hope so," Rory replied with a slight smirk. "After two years, you owe me."

Alice shoved him into the kitchen, where they joined the other two.

"Where did you two run off to, then?" Mary asked as they took seats at the round kitchen table.

"Went for a walk. We had quite a bit of catching up to do," Rory said, planting a kiss on Mary's pale, chapped lips.

"I'll say," Mary replied, smiling. "Dex has been filling me in all about his internship. It sounds very prestigious."

"Oh, believe me, I know how important and prestigious Dex's internship is," Rory replied, smirking.

"Really?" Dex laughed. "You mean every letter I sent you emphasized it enough?"

"Shut it, you," Rory teased.

"So, Alice, tell me all about your new job," Mary said, turning toward her.

"Oh, well, it was just an interview. I don't know if I've got it yet," Alice said, slightly flustered. "But it's for a primary school in London. That way Dex and I would be able to find a place together in the city."

"That's great," Mary said, sincerely. "How do you think the interview went?"

Alice wasn't used to Mary having this much interest in her. "I think it went well. I really hit it off with the headmaster. I just hope my CV supports my cause," she laughed.

"I do too," Mary said politely.

Four hours and a few drinks later, the friends were huddled around the fireplace in the living area.

"So, no heat in your cottage, eh?" Dex said, his teeth chattering, his arms encompassing Alice with a quilt draped over the two of them. "Not a luxury we can afford, mate," Rory replied, his own arms sheltering Mary from the cold. The two of them were covered head to toe in hand knitted winter gear.

"We told you two to dress warmly," Mary said, pleasantly.

"How are you two not freezing your arses off right now?" Alice managed, teeth gritted tightly.

Mary laughed. "I suppose we're just used to it by now."

"You know, if you're struggling," Dex began, "I'm willing to lend you a few pounds."

"But we're not," Rory replied, smiling. "We've got so used to living without, that we simply don't miss it any more." He said it so vaguely that Dex couldn't help but wonder what else the newly-weds were "living without."

"What's on the agenda for tomorrow, then?" Alice asked Mary.

"Well, Rory usually sleeps in, but it being Sunday I'll go to the church down the road for their worship service. Then the neighbors across the field usually have us over for stew."

"Right," Alice said. "I forgot it was Sunday."

"You're welcome to come with me," Mary said. "Rory used to, but since he's supposed to be resting more anyway, he's been staying at home for the past few weeks. You're welcome too, Dex," Mary gestured toward him.

"That's alright, Mary," Dex replied. "I think I'll be nursing a slight hangover tomorrow morning."

"How much have you had to drink tonight?" Rory said with a laugh.

Dex reached for the bottle of wine in the middle of the circle.

"Not enough for this conversation," he laughed.

Mary giggled. "No judgment for not wanting to join me, Dex. What about you, Alice?"

Alice opened her mouth, but before she could respond, Rory interrupted. "It's been a while since you two have spent any girl time, just the two of you," he said. "It might be fun."

"Yeah, but that's not what it is, is it?" Alice replied. "It's not girl time, it's going to church."

"I'd still really enjoy your company," Mary insisted with a smile.

After a pause, Alice finally said, "Sure, why not." She was unable to hide her lack of enthusiasm. "They're not going to make me do a strange chant or join in on some animal sacrifice, are they?"

"They did away with all that after the uprising from the elders,"

Mary joked, as Rory mouthed to Alice, "Thank you."

Alice was still deep in REM sleep, being spooned by Dex who was keeping her warm by the fire, when she was shaken awake by Mary.

"It's time to get going, Al," Mary whispered, careful not to wake Dex.

"Seriously," muttered Alice, groggily. "It's so early."

"It's a bit of a walk," Mary said cheerily. "Best be off!"

Alice unraveled herself from Dex's broad arms and, half-awake, she pulled on a red jumper over a black dress and tights, and strapped on her Oxfords. She then followed Mary, who was wearing a similar outfit, although with more vibrant colors, and accessorized with a gray wooly hat to cover her bald head, out of the door and into the cool, damp air of dawn.

The two young women traipsed down the cobblestone road, the same path Alice took just the day before with Rory. She was still waking up and therefore was not as conversational as Mary.

"Sleep well?" Mary asked her. And without waiting for a response, "I apologize again for making you and Dex crash in the living room. I hope the fire kept you warm. I am certain that any excuse to encase yourself in that piece of man candy is welcomed, though. So I don't feel too terrible about it."

Alice snorted. It was times like this when she was able to think of Mary as a friend, and not simply a Jesus freak who stole her best friend away. It reminded her of old times.

Alice and Mary strolled down the cobblestone road that connected the cottage to civilization for ten minutes before coming upon a beautiful, old church. The greenery surrounding the chapel was sprinkled with tombstones, all dating back to the eighteenth century. Mary led Alice up the footpath to the entrance of the church, where the priest was there greeting the congregation.

"Mary!" cried the minister. "Good morning!"

"Good morning, Father Richard," Mary replied, smiling.

"You couldn't get Rory out of bed, yet again?" chuckled the minister. "But I see you brought a guest with you!"

"Yes, this is my friend Alice," Mary pulled Alice to her side. "She and Rory's brother Dex are staying with us for a few days."

"Brilliant!" roared Father Richard. His round belly shook with enthusiasm. "Well, come on in, loves. It's lovely to have you, Alice."

"Thank you," Alice replied rather shyly.

Mary linked arms with Alice and led her friend into the quaint sanctuary. To Alice's apprehension, Mary walked straight up to the front row and sat down in one of the blue chairs that had been organized in rows for the congregation to sit. Alice thought they looked out of place in the medieval atmosphere of the church; she had expected her bum to go numb on hard, wooden benches. But the chairs were quite comfortable. Alice just hoped that she wouldn't fall asleep during the service.

The organist, hidden from view behind the instrument, was playing a soft and classical piece, one which did not help Alice's efforts to remain awake. Soon enough, the priest glided to the front and took his place behind the pulpit.

"Welcome," Father Richard said as he raised his arms, his palms facing the ceiling. "This is the day that the Lord has made."

"We will rejoice and be glad in it," chorused twenty voices from the chairs. Alice whipped her head around, caught off guard. Mary pointed out the call and response on the piece of paper that had been given to her by an elderly man on her way to her seat. She followed along, though did not read aloud like the others. Alice did not necessarily believe in Heaven or Hell, but she believed in sacredness. And she was not about to anger a God by saying things about which she had no basis of understanding.

Mary, on the other hand, carried her voice the loudest. Not only with call and response, but with hymns as well. Alice realized that there was quite a bit of standing and sitting, standing and sitting when it came to church. They stood when people would read from certain parts of the Bible, but remained seated for others. They stood for the hymns but sat for the prayers. Alice quite enjoyed standing next to Mary, hearing her angelic voice carry the tunes of the hymns. After the priest's sermon, they all stood for the remaining hymn.

Alice glanced over Mary's shoulder at the correct page in the hymn book, so that it would at least look as though she was participating. But as the song began and Alice followed along with the lyrics, the most amazing thing happened. Alice began to weep.

It was silent, and no one noticed, not even Mary. But as Alice listened to the words and saw Mary, her eyes closed and one hand balancing the hymn book, the other raised up to the ceiling, as though wanting to be called on by a teacher, Alice was overcome with inexplicable emotion.

As Mary sang the last chorus with gusto, Alice could not help but join in. The volume inside the church began to build at the last line, and an incredible vibrato carried throughout the sanctuary.

The last note rang out, and the organist let it hold for at least eight full beats. After the music ended, the congregants cried, "Amen!" In that moment, Alice understood. She may not have accepted the values and beliefs that Mary did, but she finally accepted why Mary was the way she was. How she could stand there, her head bald from chemotherapy, wrapped in a scarf, her cardigan swamping her frail, pale body, and sing and praise the God she knew and so heartily believed in. And for the first time, Alice was jealous of Mary for a reason that had nothing to do with Rory. She was jealous of her faith and comfort in something so powerful that even a disease that was literally killing her could not take away her joy.

Fourteen

Rory had come to open Mary's letters more and more cautiously. He did not approach them with the same childlike enthusiasm, but rather with hesitation.

Hello Darling,

By now you are probably properly annoyed with me. But that's okay, you have every right to be. But let me just warn you that you're going to be even more irritated with me after this next task. Remember that one time I wanted to get a tattoo on my torso? I wanted my favorite Bible verse, but you said that tattoos were ugly. You said that you didn't understand why I would inflict more pain on myself than my illness already had. I appreciated that, so I never got one. So now I seek my revenge. Muahaha! Just joking, love. Well, not really. I want you and Alice to go to the tattoo parlor on Baker Road. It's near their flat. I know because Alice dragged me there when she got her belly button pierced. Go with her and get something –anything — to have something permanent in your life for once. If you didn't follow the instructions from my last letter, I'm doubtful you will heed these wishes. But a girl can hope that her husband would be willing to challenge himself, to commit to something even when his last commitment failed him. If nothing else, it will probably make Alice very, very happy.

Love, your Mary.

If Rory were to be completely honest with himself, he would admit that this was not the worst task Mary could have made him do. True, he despised tattoos. He thought they were ugly, and he had been stuck with needles enough in his life involuntarily, no way would he go through it by choice.

Even with this mindset, ten minutes later he found himself and Alice walking toward Baker Road, Alice giving suggestion after suggestion of what he should get inked onto his body.

"Oh, you should get a lower back tattoo! That way no one sees it but you. And it's funny."

"Alice, I'm not getting a lower back tattoo," Rory said bluntly. "I'm getting the smallest, cheapest possible option and that's that."

"Oh, yeah, because that's sexy," Alice sneered, rolling her eyes.

"Sexier than a lower back tattoo?"

"Come on Rory, I've been begging Dex to get a tattoo to match the one on my shoulder. You know, the half of the heart one? Maybe you should get the other half, make him jealous, and then he'll finally do it!"

"What is it with girlfriends blackmailing their boyfriends into getting tattoos?" Rory asked incredulously. "Since when did guys start behaving like strict fathers who don't want their daughters ruining their bodies?"

"Okay, first of all," replied Alice, "do not ever insinuate that Dex is my father. That's just…Ew. Secondly, we're here." The shop was smaller than Alice and Dex's flat, and Rory immediately regretted his decision to follow through with this. Getting a tattoo would not change anything in his or Mary's relationship. It wouldn't bring her back to life. It wouldn't save him, as Mary had tried and failed to do so many times.

Alice swung the door open and steered her fearful male

companion inside. Rory glanced around the place.

"I feel like we'll be leaving here with something other than tattoos," Rory whispered. "Like hepatitis."

Alice elbowed him in his ribs as a very prominently pierced and tatted man emerged from a room separated from the rest of the store only by a curtain.

"Can I help you?" he asked, his voice not matching his appearance. Rory expected a husky growl, or a hiss at the very least.

But his tone was rather quite friendly, and Rory was oddly put at ease.

"Yes," Alice said assertively before Rory could say anything.

"My friend here would like a tattoo."

"What kind of tattoo are you looking for, mate?" the artist asked.

Rory shook his head. "I dunno."

"Well, we've got a lot of options in our book if you want to come and have a look."

Rory and Alice pored over the three-ring binder, which contained laminated page after page of black and colored designs. Finally, Rory landed on one of a pair of angel's wings.

"I approve!" cried Alice. "Manly, yet it has sentimental meaning."

"Sentimental meaning?" the artist asked curiously.

Alice shot a sideways glance toward Rory.

"It's in memory of my wife," Rory explained.

"Oh," the artist said understandingly. "Yeah, we get a lot of that here. Come on, then." He picked up the book and disappeared behind

the curtain. Rory followed suit, Alice behind him. Rory spun around.

"Actually, Al, you mind waiting out here?" He left his friend in the lobby and disappeared as well.

Twenty minutes later Rory emerged.

"Let's see it!" Alice exclaimed.

"There's nothing to see," Rory said flatly. "I couldn't go through with it. Backed out. I was right, tattoos are disgusting."

"Rude," commented the tattoo artist as he emerged as well.

"What?" Alice was disappointed. "But you picked out a great design! You already paid for it!"

"Look, just drop it, okay?" Rory took Alice by the crook of her elbow and steered her out of the shop.

Later that evening Rory turned into bed early. As he peeled his shirt off, he cringed. He went to the mirror and stared at his reflection. He felt the tenderness on his chest just below his collarbone. It was still red, and he was careful not to touch it. But there it was, plain as day.

Etched in jet-black ink, the name Hayden.

Summer, 2010

The sound of Mary retching into the toilet was nothing new to Rory. What was new was the amount she had been vomiting lately. It had been the third day in the row that Rory had awoken to Mary already sick in the bathroom right off the bedroom in their quaint cottage.

"Maybe we should call your uncle, Mare," Rory suggested as

his wife stumbled back into bed, her night shirt matted to her back with sweat. Even on her worst days, she was the most beautiful woman he knew.

"It's just the drugs," Mary said. "There's bound to be side effects, that's the whole point of this trial. To find out what they are."

"Yeah, but you've been sick like this for a while, and it's starting to concern me."

Mary waved Rory's comment away with a careless hand as she turned back into her pillow to go to sleep. It didn't last long though, and soon enough she was vomiting over the side of the bed, unable to make it to the bathroom in time.

"That's it," declared Rory, hastily rushing to Mary's side of the bed. "I'm calling Dr. Matthews."

Mary, too weak to respond, only nodded, and consented to letting Rory position her like a rag doll back in bed.

The waiting was always the worst. No matter if it was for treatment appointments, follow-ups, or anything else. The anticipation was overwhelming. This time, the two were waiting to see Mary's uncle, Dr. Matthews. Mary was sitting on the side of the examination table in a gown that opened at the back, her feet dangling off. Rory sat hunched over in the chair next to her, face in his hands. If Mary hadn't been so keenly aware of Rory's lack of belief in a higher power, she would have thought he was praying.

The nurse had poked, jabbed, and prodded at Mary when they first got there, taking multiple blood samples and examining her from head to toe so that hopefully, when the doctor finally saw them, he would have some answers. Mary didn't want to be taken out of the trial, though. And that was her biggest fear.

After what seemed like a lifetime, they heard a rapping of knuckles on the wooden door.

"Come in," Mary invited. Dr. Matthews, or as he was known to Mary, Uncle Fred, entered holding a clipboard and a somber expression.

"Don't say it," Mary warned him. "Don't tell me that I'm no longer a viable candidate for the trial."

Fred shook his head. "Mary, that's not at all what I'm about to tell you. Please, I just need you to listen. You too, Rory." He looked over as Rory uncovered his face and sat up a little straighter. "Mary," Fred began, "what is your current form of birth control?"

Mary stared at him. "What sort of question is that, Uncle Fred?"

Fred held up a hand. "Please, dear, I'm sorry, but I need to know."

"Condoms," Mary said bluntly. "I was taken off the pill by my GP back home because they believed it was messing with my hormones and contributing to my depression. But Rory and I are careful. More than careful. This one won't even touch me if it's even close to being time for me to start." She said the last part with disdain. Rory rolled his eyes. He would have been offended, but she said most everything with a tone of indifference nowadays, so he was not all that surprised.

"Why do you need to know this, Fred?" Rory asked. He wasn't sure he wanted to know the answer.

Fred took a sheet off of the clipboard he was holding. "You answered that your last period was nine weeks ago."

"Yeah, but that's normal for me. What with every med I've been put on and whatnot. Fred, please don't tell me what I think you're about to."

"Your blood test results revealed that you're pregnant, Mary," Fred told her.

Mary stared at him. She didn't say anything. Rory, however, had a lot to say.

"Wait-what-she's-Mary!" Rory's eyes glistened and spilled over. "Mary, this is a miracle!" He stood up and wrapped his arms around his wife, burying his head in her shoulder. Mary returned the embrace, but not the sentiment. Her face remained expressionless as she continued to stare at her uncle.

"Isn't this amazing?' Rory cried, looking at Mary, holding her at arm's length. Mary still said nothing and held her lips tightly together.

Finally, Fred spoke.

"Rory, while childbirth in any circumstance is undoubtedly a miracle, with Mary's condition, carrying a child is extremely risky not only to Mary, but to the baby as well."

"Of course it is," Rory responded. "But you're going to give us the medicine, the instructions, the foods, everything we need to do to have this baby, right?"

Mary spoke before Fred could respond, "What are the odds?"

Rory looked from her to Fred. "Wait, Mary, why aren't you happy about this? All you've wanted is to get married and have a family. We eloped, and now this is happening. It's all coming together!

That's been your dream—-"

"No, Rory," Mary interrupted. "That's been your dream. That's been your dream since we started our lives over here. And so now I'm asking you," she indicated to Fred, "not as my uncle, but as my doctor…what are the odds that my baby would survive to birth?"

Fred looked Mary in the eye and took her hand. "The odds

are not good for the baby, Mary. And the chances of your own survival are even worse. My sweet girl, your body is already trying, with every ounce of fight it has in it, to demolish the cancer cells before they kill you. Even if the two of you survived the next seven months, there is no telling the number of deformities or disabilities your baby would have."

Mary nodded as she fought back tears. How stupid, she thought, to be upset over something that never was. Or that never would be. It's why she stopped dreaming about traveling to all of those faraway places a long time ago. It's why she stopped trying to cure Rory of his bitterness. In turn, he began to compensate for the both of them. She tried getting rid of her travel books; they were only a painful reminder of dreams that she never really had the right to have. But Rory found them and stored them in their attic.

"Mary and Rory," Fred continued, "there is a decision that you two need to make. The fetus is putting an enormous amount of stress on your body. I understand if you two need time to talk, but time is not exactly on your side. It is short notice, but I can schedule an appointment for you downstairs for today."

"Wait," Rory choked. "You're not suggesting abortion?"

"Rory, it's the best option to save Mary's life."

Rory slowly nodded. He turned away as a sob escaped from his throat.

"No way," Mary said firmly.

"Mary," Fred began. "Listen to me-"

"No, Uncle Fred, you listen to me." Her eyes flashed. "I know you think I'm naïve for believing that there is a reason for everything. Not that everything happens for a reason — there's a difference. And I know that you think God is an imaginary friend for the idiots of the world —your words, not mine — but my beliefs are literally the only things I have left that belong to me. Even Rory isn't permanent in my life. He's as much on borrowed time as I am. But I know that what you're suggesting to do is wrong for me."

Rory intervened. "Er, Fred, could you give us a minute to talk about this?"

"Of course." Fred turned to leave. He hesitated at the door. "Mary, you know that this is up to you. I cannot persuade you one way or the other. But sweetheart, I just want you to know all of the facts. No matter how hard they are to hear."

Mary nodded, and Fred left them to have privacy.

Rory pulled up his chair so that he was facing Mary. "Mary, are you insane?"

"No, Rory, I'm dying. Even with this treatment I'm on, who knows how much time it's buying me!"

"But...It's killing you."

"He."

"What?"

"He. Or she. Not it. This is our baby, Rory. I cannot do what it is you're asking me to do. I understand that, in so many cases, it is right to go through with this. That so many women need to go through with it in order to survive. But I'm dying anyway, Rory. Those women know their bodies, and I know mine."

Rory buried his face in his hands. "You're right. Oh, but... Mary. How are we supposed to even dream about having a baby when he or she may have to be raised by strangers?"

"Strangers? You don't think that Dex and Alice would let this little one go anywhere besides with them, do you?"

Rory smiled. "Mary, I don't want to get our hopes up."

"I'm not getting an abortion, Rory. That's final. Sometimes I wish you understood my faith in its entirety, Rory, rather than just tolerating it."

"I have faith too, Mary!" Rory took her hands. "Faith in us!"

"But I won't always be here, Rory!"

"So?"

"So, how am I supposed to live up to everything you've entrusted to me when I'm not going to be here forever? I'm only human, Rory."

Rory had no answer. He hadn't been raised like Mary had. His family never went to church. They never prayed, and they definitely didn't say God's name in the home unless it was in vain. It was the only thing about Rory's family that made Mary uncomfortable.

So, instead of giving an answer, he asked a question. "What would the name be?"

"What?"

"Come on," Rory grinned. "Every girl dreams of what she wants to name her children. I know because Alice used to change her mind all the time about what she'd name hers and Dex's. Mind you, this was before they even started dating."

Mary laughed. "Hayden."

Rory looked thoughtfully at her. "*Hayden*. I like it. It's fitting whether the baby's a girl or boy."

"Precisely," Mary said.

Six days, nine hours, and thirty-six minutes later, Mary woke up from a restless sleep with a start. Something felt wet, and as she looked under the covers, she saw she was lying in a pool of her own blood.

"Rory!" Mary screamed.

Rory woke immediately. "What? What is it?"

But Mary couldn't speak, for she was sobbing too hard. She

doubled over in pain, her abdomen feeling like something was trying to break through. Rory leaped out of bed and reached for his mobile to alert the hospital that they were on their way. Mary couldn't walk, so Rory lifted her into his arms and laid her in the back of the car they shared. He had grabbed blankets on the way out the door and laid them over the seats, but knew there was no way to prevent the fact that they would always be reminded that there would never be a tiny person in the back of the car, only red bloodstains.

They arrived at A&E in under ten minutes, and Mary was seen quickly after. The news was not a surprise to them — she was having a miscarriage. While Mary's sobs rang out through the hospital over the loss of her child, Rory grilled the physician on call to tell them if Mary's condition would worsen. The physician told the two of them that he was going to keep Mary overnight, and once the bleeding was under control, he would do a CT scan. Then they would be released.

The doctor left them to themselves after that. Rory was at a loss for words. He had always been able to comfort Mary, and Mary him.

But he didn't know how to console Mary when he was experiencing the same loss. He always thought it would be one of them grieving the unimaginable alone. Never did he imagine they would go through it together.

Present Day

Rory never told anyone, not even Dex or Alice, about Hayden. It was a secret Mary took with her to the grave, and Rory would do the same. A secret only lives as long as there are two people to share it, after all.

Rory had gotten more and more lethargic after the tattoo

incident. He considered the possibility that it was infected, but he knew better. His symptoms could more accurately be attributed to the fact that it had been twenty-seven days since he had stopped having his chemotherapy. Yes, the nausea and vomiting had subsided (he was now indulging in every delicacy Alice whipped up), but his body was deteriorating due to the unstoppable reproductive cancer cells that plagued him. He had neglected to go to his last doctor's appointment. He didn't need a professional telling him he probably wouldn't last as long as two months any more. He was well enough in tune with his body to know this for himself.

Rory knew there was only one letter left. He could not bring himself to open the last one, not yet. He honestly had thought that Mary's letters would last him until his final days. He had been anxious not to miss one before his time came. They had given him something to live for. Now that they were nearly gone, he did not know what he was living for. Dex and Alice were already gaining closure, and he no longer felt Mary's lingering presence.

One afternoon, Rory was sitting around in his pajamas eating a chocolate spread and raspberry sandwich, when he had an urge to open his nightstand table and open the last letter, but didn't. It was not the time, not yet. Surely after the last one was read, he would fall back into the dark hole that encompassed him after Mary's death, and this time neither Alice nor Dex would be able to save him. So he restrained this compulsion. In an act that he figured he could account to pure boredom, he instead reached for the untouched Bible that lay as a decoration on the coffee table in the living room.

Immediately, Rory felt foolish. He hadn't a clue what he was supposed to do. He knew the Bible was separated into different books; Mary often quoted from them, but Rory had never been formally educated on its teachings.

I have no right even touching this thing, Rory thought. Mary, his beautiful Mary, knew lines from this book by heart, was selfless, and possessed undying faithfulness. Rory had placed his faith in Mary, and she was right. She was no longer there with him. Not of her own accord, but that did not make him feel any less hopeless. Mary realized her own mortality as well as Rory's. Is that why she placed her trust so highly in God? Rory didn't even know if he believed in God (or any higher power for that matter). In a way, he was always jealous that Mary had put God before himself. Like it had been a competition that he would never win.

He figured he was not the only person in history to not know what to do when he had a Bible in his hands. So he opened it. It landed on a page headed with the title Leviticus. He attempted to read the first paragraph and was at a total loss. So he flipped further toward the middle of the Bible. This time he landed on a page from the book of Psalms. He had heard Mary quote enough Psalms in his lifetime that he felt semi-comfortable to explore the next few pages. He even recognized some of the phrases he caught, such as Psalm 3:

Lord, how many are my foes!
How many rise up against me!
Many are saying of me,
"God will not deliver him." But you, Lord, are a shield around me,
my glory, the One who lifts my head high. I call out to the Lord, and
he answers me from his holy mountain.

Mary had recited that one to Rory several times. He re-read the verse. This time he read as though Mary's voice was speaking to him, her tone sweet and her rhythm like she was counting time in a piece of music. When she spoke of her faith, it was with such passion that at times Rory felt like he would have been moved if it wasn't for his stubbornness. He read and re-read it. And then he flipped through the book of Psalms looking for familiar verses he had heard Mary say. It was as if her letters hadn't stopped.

Rory lost track of time. He spent the next few hours leafing through Psalms, looking for familiar lines that he had heard Mary recount. But, as the night grew darker, Rory found himself reading intently, not wanting to miss a single line in case it too had escaped from Mary's lips. What Rory soon discovered was that there were many different verses in the book of Psalms. They were parts of songs, songs that were written out of love. That, Rory could appreciate. The reason he and Mary had any common ground on the basis of spirituality was the fact that Mary likened God to love itself. She would tell Rory that God was love, if love was a person. Until he met Mary, Rory did not believe in love. His parents certainly didn't show it toward each other, and his relationship with Dex wasn't all that affectionate. But with Mary, he could see what love looked like. This all-consuming, life-giving love that she claimed existed was evident through her.

Before Rory knew it, the sun was coming up through the window in the lounge. The pages glowed, basking in the sunlight. He had not finished the book, but knew that he needed to sleep. When he woke up, he would spend the rest of the day searching for verses Mary had recited. That's how he justified it to himself, anyhow.

He carried the Bible with him to his bed and put it in the

nightstand table, resting it on top of the manila envelope. He knew Alice and Dex wouldn't be missing it anytime soon.

Alice rapped her knuckles on Rory's door. She pressed her ear against the door and, after hearing no response, she quietly opened it. Rory had covered himself up to the chin with his covers, no doubt suffering from a bout of chills in the middle of the night. Alice approached the bed, but a foul, stale odor caught her off guard. She glanced down at the bed, where Rory was curled up in a fetal position, to find a damp, dark circle in the middle of the comforter.

"Dex," Alice called out. "Dex, come quick."

Rory began to stir from his deep slumber. "Alice?" he mumbled. He opened his eyes and suddenly bolted upright. He glanced down at his sheets. "No," he groaned.

Just then Dex came in. "What's happened?"

Alice approached him. "He's just pissed himself," she whispered.

Rory had slumped back into bed and covered his face with his hands.

"No," he kept repeating. "This isn't happening."

"Alice, I've got this," said Dex, eyeing his brother. "Why don't you go and fetch some clean sheets?"

Alice nodded and left, closing the door behind her.

Rory sat up and swung his legs over the side of the bed.

"Oh, no you don't," warned Dex, rushing to his side.

"Dex, I beg you to leave me alone," Rory's voice shook. He held up his palm to his brother without looking at him. "Just let me be." Dex didn't say anything. Instead, he took his brother under the arm and hoisted him out of bed. The two walked to the toilet and Dex sat Rory down on the closed lid.

"Stay put," Dex instructed, and he left the room. "Not many places I can go," called Rory.

Dex returned with clean pants, trousers, and a jumper. Dex knew there was no dignified way of changing another man. He had plenty of experience of doing the same thing with male patients at the hospital from his days of interning to know this. Rory was avoiding eye contact, silently submitting to his brother's care as he helped him get undressed.

After Rory was sorted, Alice tapped on the door to the toilet. "Alright in there?"

"Yeah, come on in," Dex replied.

Alice opened the door and kneeled down next to Rory. "Bed's taken care of," she said matter-of-factly. Rory, still too humiliated to look at either of them, nodded curtly.

"Remember that time Alice laughed so hard on the tube that she pissed herself?" Dex blurted out. Alice nodded vigorously.

"Thanks, but this is not precisely the same thing," Rory murmured.

"No, seriously, I thought that I was going to die of embarrassment," Alice insisted. "Literally the worst day. And if I recall correctly, it was all your fault, Ror. You're the one who made me laugh!"

"At least you were able to clean yourself after, yes?" Rory snarled. "Sorry, Alice." He shook his head. "There's just not a way to spin this. I know you mean well, but this is about as low as it gets."

"I know, Ror," Alice conceded. "But I need you to realize that we don't see you differently. You took care of Mary when she got to this point. You didn't look at her differently, did you?"

"Mary was my wife, of course I didn't," Rory said. "I loved her…I would have done anything for her."

"So you didn't think anything of it, then, did you?" asked Dex.

"No," said Rory.

"That gives you a taste of how we feel about you," said Alice.

Rory felt his throat close up. He couldn't speak. "Why didn't you let me end this before it got this far?" he choked out. "I knew that this would be my fate if my disease progressed. Well, it did, and look at me! This pathetic thing that I don't even recognize. How could you let this happen?"

Alice's face contorted with emotion. "Because you wouldn't have been able to experience the joy of Mary's letters before you left us," she insisted.

Rory nodded. He aggressively rubbed his eyes and looked down at her, so small and folded in on herself on the tiled floor. He could have sworn that as he began wasting away, his best friend had as well. He couldn't help but remember watching Mary going through her last days, when he felt like he was disintegrating from the inside out. "I just want to go back to sleep," he whispered, his voice cracking.

Alice nodded. "Alright, love. Come on then." She stood up with an outstretched arm. Rory picked himself up and went to her, allowing her to lead him to his bedroom. His eyes still burned and his body was shaking from rage and humiliation. He crawled under his covers and turned away from Alice.

Dex approached him from behind with a red, round tablet.

"Take this," he said. "It's melatonin; it'll help you fall asleep quicker."

Rory took the tiny pill, sure it would not help him much, but thanked Dex nonetheless. After he took a sip of water from the glass Dex offered him, he turned back over without another word.

Alice and Dex took this as their cue to leave. They let Rory be, and did not re-enter his bedroom after they had closed the door, even after they heard the sounds of muffled sobs coming from within.

Alice was the one to finally reach into the manila envelope and retrieve the remaining letter. She handed Rory the letter as he ate his breakfast in bed the next morning.

"Alice, no, it isn't time yet," Rory argued.

"Yes, it is," Alice replied firmly. "Rory, I know that you think that after you read Mary's last letter, you'll feel as though she's died all over again. But rest assured that it will bring you more comfort right now than despair, alright?"

Rory nodded and accepted the small white envelope from her slightly shaking hands. He set it on his nightstand and continued to eat his breakfast.

Alice turned without another word and let her friend be, trusting her instinct that he would give in to the lure.

As soon as Alice shut the door, Rory ripped open the envelope, taking out a single sheet with cursive writing taking up the front and back of the page. He ran his fingers absentmindedly over the words, and had to nearly cover up the entire page as he started reading so as not to be tempted to skip ahead.

Dear Rory,

When I was ten years old, my parents surprised me for my birthday. They told me we were going on a trip, somewhere I had never been before. I had just recently become obsessed with the Massacre of Glencoe and had brought along my four-hundred-page book with me in hopes that the train we were going on would lead us to that destination. Well, it did not. It took us to Edinburgh. I pretended to be excited, but I'm sure my parents saw right through it. They pretended to be sad that I had got my hopes up for something, and that I was not pleased with my surprise.

Then, as we were walking, we arrived at a rather large bus labeled Highland Experience. My father pulled out three tickets and told me that we were going on a tour of the Highlands, including Glencoe! I don't think I could have screamed louder if I had tried. Mind you, I was in my third round of treatment at this point, so I was astonished that they had planned a trip this far, much less a tour of the Highlands. But they assured me that it was the sort of tour I could handle, seeing as we would be on a bus for most of it.

Well, twelve hours later I had traveled up to Glencoe, Loch Ness, and then to Inverness. Although I was sitting on a bus for nearly the entirety of the journey, I was exhausted by the end. But let me tell you something about the Highlands, Rory. You feel like you are on another planet, like Mars or something. You feel as though you are so distant from the world and its gadgets, its conflicts and problems. There is so much history there of violence and destruction, but all you feel is peace by the openness and vast space of it all. My parents carried me all the way to the train station that night, I was overcome with fatigue, but I was also the happiest ten-year-old on the planet that day.

While it was the most beautiful voyage I have taken to this day,

I do hold regrets in my heart about it. As the bus drove through Glencoe, I peered out of my window and basked in the sunlit greenery that went up and down, up and down with each rolling hill. I saw the tops of the Munros from a distance, and all I could think of was, "I want to climb those." I wanted to be that high over the world, to look down and see people as small as ants. If people were that small, can you imagine how small our problems would be? Maybe they would still be as big as us. It's all a matter of perspective I guess.

Anyhow, Rory, I think you know what I'm getting at. This is the last letter I'm writing to you. I want you to know how badly I wanted to climb this mountain. I dreamt about it for years after. I never told a soul, not in fear of being made fun of or anything of that sort. But because I was afraid that if I spoke of it out loud, then it would be real. And then it would be unattainable. Kept secretly in my mind, at least it was still reachable. But Rory, this is reachable for you. Because you have nothing left to lose, my dear. I know that this is asking more of you than anything before. I don't care if you didn't steal from the shop, or never made amends with your mother. None of that matters when it comes to this final wish. That you would experience what it is like to be larger than your illness, rather than what it feels like for your illness to be larger than you.

I've been thinking long and hard about what I want to say in my last letter to you. I know that I must choose my words carefully, as it takes a long time for me to do the simplest activities now, including writing. So what I can think of is this: Love convicts. If it didn't, then it would not be true. It convicts us of our most terrible qualities, of our most sinful nature. But love also offers grace. We don't deserve this grace, but love offers it unconditionally.

1 John 4:16 states that God is Love. The love that I've shown you comes from God, Ror. All real love does. How else do we forgive the unforgivable? To hope to repair a relationship when it is beyond broken? If I offered you myself, if I served you as a wife should, if I spoke nothing but good things to you every day and only did right by you, but did so without love, then it would have no meaning at all.

This love is redeeming, renewing, and powerful. It takes our burdens and carries them so that we don't have to. It saves us from ourselves. I think I first made this revelation in the Highlands. I want so badly for you to experience this ecstatic beauty for yourself, in the realest sense possible. Not from a tour bus below, but from above, at the highest point. But do not do this for me, Rory. Do it for yourself.

I love you.

And wherever I am, know that I am missing you.

Your Mary

When Rory entered the kitchen, he found Dex poring over a medical textbook, and Alice writing up lesson plans. She was planning a craft and, by the example she had made, Rory could tell her five-year-olds would be leaving school tomorrow utterly covered in glitter.

Rory tossed pages of the Munros of Glen Coe that he printed out using Alice's laptop and printer onto the kitchen table, narrowly missing Alice's creation.

"Oi, watch it!" she exclaimed.

"What's that?" Dex asked, glancing up from his material.

"It's Mary's last request for me," Rory responded. "The last letter. She wants me to climb a Munro in the Highlands and experience the...uh...'ecstatic beauty' or whatever."

"The Highlands as in Scotland?" Dex said incredulously.

"But Rory," Alice half-laughed. "You hate nature. And anything that may be construed as beautiful."

Rory snickered. "True. But I think this is something I actually want to do. Mary wrote of this place with such enthusiasm. I want to experience what she was trying to make me understand."

Dex and Alice exchanged hesitant looks with each other. Rory did not notice. He continued talking about his plans.

"Anyway, I figured we could go up there this weekend. It's only about a four-hour train ride to Edinburgh, then maybe a few more to drive up to Glen Coe—-"

"Hold up there," Dex interrupted. "Ror, look, I'm sorry mate, but I have to work this weekend. And Alice has to prepare for next week's parent-teacher meetings this weekend.

Rory stared at them. Of course, their lives did not revolve around him. It may have felt that way at first, right after he had moved in. But Rory was not the center of their lives anymore. Just like he had wanted.

Still, he wondered why this disappointed him.

"Alright then," Rory said after he had recovered from the initial shock of his friends' unavailability. "I'll go by myself."

Alice snorted. Rory turned to glare at her.

"What?"

"You can't be serious! Rory, you can't even make it five minutes on the tube without throwing up. And need I remind you what happened just the other day? How do you expect to make it up a mountain, even with Dex and me, much less you on your own?"

"Look, I have faith that Mary thinks I can do it. And I have my faith in other things too. It's complicated…But I know I can do it. Mary knows I can do it. Why else would she ask me to, knowing I wouldn't refuse anything she asked of me?"

Dex closed his textbook and leaned across the table. "Mary didn't know what state you'd be in by this time, Rory. Why did you never offer to take her hill climbing? Were you too weak?"

"No, she was."

Dex gave him a knowing look.

"I was also really selfish," Rory blurted out. "And I didn't understand why Mary wanted — why she needed-to go so badly!"

"Rory, look," Alice said. "I think the fact that you're even trying to do this is a really great way to honour Mary. But if I'm being completely honest, I think that this is a really stupid idea."

Rory rounded on her. "God, Alice, why do you have to be like that all the time? You were all for publicly humiliating me with the stealing and the tattoos and making me ride carnival rides until I vomit. But when it comes to something real, something worth the effort, you just piss all over it!"

That had done it. For once, Alice didn't have a comeback.

"I know that every day I lose a little more of my dignity," Rory continued, his voice calmer. "Is it too much to ask for just a little respect from you?"

"Then give us something to respect you for!" Alice's voice cut through Rory's already broken heart like a knife.

Dex shifted his glance over at Alice. Her mouth slowly turned into an O. Once again, she had realized what she had said too late. She shook her head violently.

"No, Rory, I didn't mean—-"

But Rory was done. He snatched his papers off the table, knocking whatever in God's name Alice was working on off the table, shattering it into tiny pieces. He didn't care. He marched to his room and slammed the door.

Alice immediately rose from the table. "Rory, I didn't mean it."

But Dex gently pulled her back. "Leave him. He just needs to cool off."

Alice looked helpless. "I am a terrible person."

"No, you're not." Dex brushed a couple of strands that had come loose from Alice's bun back behind her ear. "But you shouldn't have said what you did."

"I'm just so frustrated," said Alice. "People hill climb for sport, as a hobby. People who climb a Munro have experience with this sort of thing. How could he possibly think that doing this in his condition is a good idea?"

"Because of who it's for," Dex whispered.

Alice shook her head again. "Mary," she said quietly.

Dex nodded. "Look, I agree that this is a terrible idea. But, Alice, I think you sometimes forget that you are not his mother."

"I'm well aware that I am not Rory's mother!" Alice replied, rather defensively.

"Sometimes you're a little controlling of his life, and a bit overprotective. And I know you probably feel like you have earned that right because you're one of the people who has known him like this the longest. But you're not responsible for his life."

"Well, someone has to be!"

"Look, it's not your place. He's my brother."

"Yeah, and he's my best friend." Alice sat down again at the kitchen table. "He always has been. At times, he was my only friend. So excuse me, Dex, for trying my best to keep him around as long as possible."

Dex held out his hand as an offering to Alice. She accepted it, and he pulled her up into his arms. He held her in an embrace that reminded Alice of the old days. The days when Rory was going for a test or a scan, and they would wait at the Gallaghers' for him. Sometimes she would come over to the house, her anxiety pouring out of her in sobs, because she couldn't stand the uncertainty of the future for her friend. And they would hold each other.

"I know it, love," Dex whispered into her ear. "I know everything. And as someone who has known Rory the longest, you should realize that his stubborn heart is going to do whatever it pleases, no matter what anyone else says."

He pulled her away and held her at arms' length. "Even if those people happen to be his best friend and his big brother."

Alice stared off into space, lost in her thoughts. Finally, she looked at Dex.

"How tall are you? I have some things in the storage I think we're going to need to get out."

Rory was attempting to read the Gospel of John when Alice and Dex opened the door. Rory was so disgruntled he did not realize what they had brought in with them.

"Don't bother knocking or anything," Rory spat.

"It's not like you'd let me come in anyway," Alice retorted. "This was just quicker."

Rory rolled his eyes. "What have you got there, then?"

Alice held it up for him to see. "It's your pack. Dex helped me realize why you want to do this."

"No shit," Rory mumbled. "These walls are paper thin. I can always hear everything you are—-"

"Don't interrupt, Ror, God," Dex cut him off. "Go ahead," he nodded at Alice.

"As I was saying," Alice continued. "I realized why you are so adamant on going on this bloody trip. And I also realized that I am doing the exact thing to you that you did to Mary. And I can see it in your eyes, how much you loathe yourself for it."

Rory looked away, unable to speak due to the lump that had formed in his throat.

"Rory," Alice took her usual seat on the foot of the bed. "It's not that I don't respect you. You know that Dex and I think you are the most courageous man we know. I was, and am, simply scared for you."

Rory nodded. "I know," he said hoarsely.

"And while we both," Alice looked up at Dex for support, "still stand by what I said…that this would be a stupid mistake…it's your stupid mistake to make."

"So you're really going to let me hike up this mountain?" Rory asked in disbelief. "All on my own?"

Dex reached into the hall and presented another, fuller, packed bag. "Hell, no."

Rory looked up at him in surprise.

"We have to make sure you make it all the way up," Dex said. If you're going through with this, you want to do it right. And make it to the top. Besides, someone is going to have to haul you up that thing when you collapse." Dex chuckled.

"This is, of course," Alice added, "unless Dex is carrying me up the entire time. Because, let's face it, I may quite possibly be less athletic than poor Rory."

All three of them laughed at that.

"But what about you having to work?" Rory asked Dex. "And you," pointing to Alice, "and your Parent-Teacher meetings?"

"I got someone to cover my shift at work," Dex explained. "I'll just work doubles next week. And Alice called every single parent and rescheduled with them after explaining the situation."

"You told those children's parents you couldn't meet with them because you had to take your boyfriend's sick brother hill climbing?" Rory asked Alice, unconvinced.

"I may or may not have said that I was merely aiding you in accomplishing your dying wish," Alice replied, blushing.

"There it is," Rory laughed.

"The point is," Dex spoke up, "we're all going. All or none, mate."

"This isn't going to be an easy trip," Rory warned. "For any of us."

"We know," Dex acknowledged.

"It could quite possibly be disastrous."

"Oh, absolutely," Alice agreed.

"So we're on, then?" Rory asked.

Dex smiled. "Definitely."

Fifteen

Rory sat in the living room with Alice's handwoven blanket wrapped around him. He did little else these days. The Bible lay on the coffee table, not forgotten, just set aside for the time being. Travel journals the Abels had sent Rory from Mary's bedroom had taken up space on the couch, which Rory had made into his living space. He ate his meals there now, and pored over brochures about hiking tips and supplies.

He reached beneath the couch's far left cushion and retrieved his box of Marlboros. He kept his lighter in the table to the right of the sofa, in the third drawer. The table only existed for the vase of flowers Alice set out but could never remember to water. So he knew no one would find it there. Not that they would care at this point, a fact that Rory didn't know relieved him or frightened the life nearly out of him.

His body was slowly betraying him. The withdrawal of the morphine he was going through so he could make this bloody trip was agonizing. His hands shook so violently that he couldn't get a proper light on his cigarette. Before he could take his frustration out on something, like throwing the lighter across the room and potentially burning down the flat, the door buzzed.

Rory got up as quickly as he could, which these days was at a turtle's pace. Cigarette dangling from his lip, he opened the door without bothering to see who it was through the peephole.

"Mum?" he whispered. The unlit cigarette fell from his mouth and silently hit the floor.

There she stood, clutching her handbag tightly, her knee-length coat buttoned all the way up to her chin.

"Hello, darling."

Rory's disbelief at the vision of his mother standing there quickly turned to disgust.

"What are you doing here? Is Dad with you?" He peered around the slight woman outside, but no one was behind her.

"No," Sarah said, her voice unsteady. "Your father...Arthur doesn't exactly know I'm here."

"And why are you here, then?" Rory had yet to close the door.

"Look," Sarah's voice was stronger this time as she spoke. She advanced past Rory, who remained grounded in his place. "I know that I have no right coming around here like this, especially at this point. But I'm going to ask you to show me the mercy you deserved from me, but I never gave you."

"That's a hell of an apology," Rory grumbled, pulling the blanket higher up around his shoulders. "You come up with that on the tube?"

Sarah stared at her son in the eye for the first time since she could remember. "Rory, please," she said softly. Not like she was begging, but rather like he was a child and had tracked mud onto the carpet. "There are things I want to say to you, and I need you to let me say them. Then you can throw me out and never have to look at me again."

Rory shut the door, a non-verbal invitation for his mother to continue. "Have a seat."

Sarah drew up a chair and sat straight across from the couch. Rory shuffled some travel books around to make space for him to fall into the cushions. He pulled out another cigarette and attempted again to light it. After several unsuccessful attempts, Sarah spoke.

"Let me help you with that, sweetheart."

"No, I've got it," Rory snapped. He continued, to no avail. Finally, he handed it to his mother. She took it and lit it for her son, all the while looking at Rory timidly. After the cigarette was finally lit, Rory took a drag from it and closed his eyes, feeling his entire body relax. Neither one of them spoke for several minutes.

Finally, Sarah broke the silence. "Rory, I am sorry."

"What for?" Rory took another drag. "I'm the one who ditched you guys. I left you, remember? Or at least that's how you and Dad saw it."

"I know you loved Mary. I understand that her family was able to provide for you when we could not. But that does not make up for the fact that you didn't let me take care of you when you needed me the most! When I needed to be your mother, if not for your sake then for mine! You turned to that girl, and you let her take my place!"

Rory realized that his mother had been waiting years to let this out. He stared at her. He always thought that it was selfish of his parents to make him feel guilty for leaving them for Wales.

"It was never my intention to make you feel that way," Rory said quietly.

"It doesn't matter, Rory. We thought we were going to lose you the first year you were diagnosed. Remember how scary the bone grafting was? And then the chemotherapy...I never dreamt of getting to see you live past your teenage years. But even though you didn't die, I still felt like I had lost my son."

Rory hung his head low. He didn't want the guilt in his eyes to spill over, much less let his mother see. "Just because I left," he managed, "didn't mean I didn't need you to be my mother any more."

"I know, my dear boy. As for your father," Sarah continued, "Rory, I know it is hard for you to believe, but he truly does love you."

Rory snorted and looked up at her. "Dad doesn't love me, Mum.

He hates me, he always has. Ever since I left."

"Your father was unable to support you financially!" Sarah exclaimed, surprising Rory. "Mary's parents gave you everything he couldn't! Rory, he didn't hate you, he hated himself. To him, you are a reminder of when he could barely get food on the table for his family. He believes he failed you in that, and it's just easier for him to act like you're already gone. He doesn't blame you for the pain that you caused this family. He blames himself."

Rory sat on that for a while. "And who do you blame?"

"I used to blame Mary. There. Is that what you wanted me to say?"

"There it is, then."

"I used to, Rory," Sarah repeated.

"What caused your sudden revelation that she is not the She-Devil who ruined your life?" Rory's sharpness caught him off guard and he realized that maybe he too had been holding in what he wanted to say to his mother for quite a long time.

Sarah didn't say anything right away. Instead, she pulled out an envelope from her bag and handed it over to Rory. It had already been opened, and the letter had been refolded and stuffed back inside.

"This is a letter she sent me. Before she died, of course. She must have known..." Sarah's voice trailed off. Rory took the envelope from his mother's slightly trembling hands and unfolded the letter inside.

Instead of Mary's usual doting greeting, it was addressed to his mother.

He read the entire thing silently before responding.

Dear Mrs. Gallagher,

Time is a precious gift, not only to the terminally ill, but the healthy as well. So let me get straight to the point. I know you hate me. You always have. And I wish I had got to know you better so I could have changed your mind about me. I think you would have liked me, if you had got to know me. I never meant to steal your son from you. Rory made the decision all on his own, and I am not saying that to place blame, but to inform you of reality. However, he never did it to spite you or your husband. He did it because he loved me, and for two people who are doomed for a tragically short life, we have to make decisions that may cost us things, if it means us getting the most out of the short amount of time we have. The fact of the matter is, Rory and I do not have much time. Time to travel, to talk, or to make amends. So I ask you, when you feel the urge in your heart to reach out to your son, take hold of that and act on it. Because Rory loves you. He missed you every day he was away from you. He wanted to be with me, but he still needed his mother. So please, please heed my words. There will come a time when I am no longer here, and Rory will be without the support he needs. The support only a mother can give her child. Know that I know that Rory is the man he is because of the love you have shown him. And for that, I am forever grateful to you.

Sincerely,

Mary

When Rory finished reading, he looked up at his mother, his eyes shining.

"Did she send one to Dad?" he asked.

"No, dear. At least, not to my knowledge. And I never showed this to your father. I'm sorry to say that your father is set in his ways. His stubbornness has got the best of him, I'm afraid. Some things are unrealistic to hope for, Rory. And unfortunately for your father, forgiving you, and himself, is one of those things."

Rory nodded his head, indicating he understood.

"Mary was a lovely girl," Sarah continued. "I wish...I wish I had got to spend more time with her. Got to know her better."

"You would have loved her."

"Yes, well," Sarah picked up her bag and stood, indicating she was ready to leave. "I truly am sorry, Rory. I was never the mother I should have been to you. Especially when you needed my support the most. I can only hope that you find some way in your heart to forgive me. Because I can't—-" Rory was startled to hear his mother's voice cracking. She took a shallow breath. "I cannot bear to know that you will die hating me." She stood straight as a board, eyes boring into his.

"Mum," Rory shook his head. "I do not, and will not ever hate you."

"I want to spend more time with you, sweetheart," Sarah reached for her son's cheek and cupped it with her hand. It felt familiar to Rory, comforting yet slightly painful. Similar to Mary's letters. "I want to see you more often. Can we have dinner sometime this weekend?" She took the crook of Rory's arm and started toward the front door.

"Oh, this weekend's no good," Rory said. "It's kind of a long story, but Dex and Alice and I are all hill climbing in Scotland."

"Oh!" Sarah was taken aback. "Are you sure...you can do that?"

"It's really important that I try."

"Why?"

"Mary sent me a letter too. Well, loads of them. All with things she wanted me to do before I...While I still can. Before I join her, you know?"

Sarah's face fell slightly, but Rory took no notice. He was getting excited again, just thinking of his upcoming trip.

"At first, the letters were odd. She had me doing what I thought were stupid, meaningless tasks. But she really taught me what it meant to, well, live." He laughed. He would have liked to talk to his mother about his recent encounter with the Bible, with Jesus, and all of his questions to which he had started searching for answers. But he didn't want to overwhelm her. He would save that conversation for dinner. "Anyway," he continued. "This mountain thing is the last thing she's asked me to do."

Sarah looked up at her son, who was taller than her. When had that happened? she wondered. Her face was full of concern, which Rory was now able to detect. His face fell. In an attempt to recover the moment, Sarah sniffed and said in a voice full of false optimism, "Well then. The Monday you return. You and I, sir, have a date. I'll come back into the city, and you can take me to one of the places all the young people hang out at."

Rory was silent for a moment. Then, "Sounds like a plan, Mum."

"I'll be looking forward to seeing you again, then."

"Me too," Rory said, his voice suddenly very serious.

Sarah cupped her son's cheek once more. "I love you,

sweetheart. Until Monday, then." With that, she quickly exited the flat, shutting the door behind her and leaving Rory alone in the hallway.

To no one, Rory muttered, "Til Monday, then."

Sixteen

The trio arrived at London's King's Cross station at nine o'clock in the morning. All three were groggy and red-eyed, having not gotten much sleep the night before. In Alice's and Dex's case, this was due to last-minute preparation and packing. In Rory's, to nerves and anxiety. Dex was carrying a pack on his back for Alice and himself, and Alice was carrying Rory's. All three of them swiped their tickets through the machine and entered through the turnstile one at a time. After looking at the overhead screen, Dex found out they would be loading at Platform 10. They walked as swiftly as they could with their baggage on their back, save Rory's inability to walk quickly without becoming overcome with fatigue.

They finally reached their platform just as their train arrived. All three of them were seated at a table, and they collapsed into their seats, storing the baggage in the overhead compartment. Rory closed his eyes and breathed in through his nose, out through his mouth.

"Alright?" Dex asked. Rory nodded.

"Never better." There were a countless number of things Rory had anticipated going awry, preventing him from getting to Scotland. He exhaled with relief knowing that he was finally on board.

The train pulled out of the station, gathering speed. Rory looked out the window at the trees blur together until they were a canvas of green. He was on his way.

Rory slept almost anywhere and at any time lately, so he had no trouble falling asleep on the train. The challenge was waking him up once they had arrived at Edinburgh Waverly train station. Alice shook his arm rather aggressively before he stirred.

"Eh?" he asked muzzily.

"Time to go, mate," Dex said, retrieving their belongings from overhead.

The train halted and the doors opened, letting an icy gust of wind into the compartment. The three friends stepped onto the platform and followed the signs for "Way Out."

As they walked up the steep steps out into the bustling city, Rory wrapped his coat around him more tightly and pulled his scarf up over his mouth. Dex walked ahead and hailed a taxi while the other two caught up.

Dex had an old friend from medical school living in Edinburgh now, working at Western General. After Dex had explained to him the nature of their visit, and that they would require a car to drive up to the Highlands, he was more than accommodating. The taxi drove them to the address Dex's friend had given him and, after a quick reunion, the three of them continued on their journey to Glen Coe.

As they would be arriving around late afternoon, they decided to rent a room at a hotel in Glen Coe near where the mountains began and begin their excursion early the next morning. It was just as well that they planned it this way, as Rory would barely keep his eyes open in the three-hour car ride to their destination.

Alice acted as navigator to Dex, who was driving. Rory was sprawled out in the back, and if safety were a concern, they would have had him sit up. But given the circumstances, they let him be. The road from the time they exited the motorway onto the road leading to the mountains was narrow and winding. Rory felt nauseated and had to ask Dex twice to pull over so he could vomit and collect himself.

"We can turn back, Rory," Alice said worriedly the second time this happened. "You've been through a lot today, and obviously the anti-nausea medicine you took isn't working. Maybe we should just find somewhere to stay around here, and see how you feel in the morning."

Rory shook his head as he closed the door to the car and lay back down on the seat. "We're on a timetable, you said so yourself. This is how I'm going to feel whether we stop or keep going, so we might as well keep on." He wiped his mouth and closed his eyes.

Alice and Dex exchanged glances with one another, and Dex shifted the car into gear, pulling back onto the road.

They drove like this for about one hundred and sixty miles before finally coming upon a sign for the Loch Leven Hotel. Alice and Dex had refrained from waking Rory, but not without extreme effort. The sights once they hit the Highlands were absolutely breathtaking. Living in the city for the past few years, they had forgotten how green and pure the world could look.

They pulled into the car park, and as Dex turned the engine off, Rory awoke with a start.

"Are we here?" he grumbled.

Alice turned around to face him. "See for yourself."

Rory propped himself up on his elbow to peer out the back window. Never in his life had he seen anything so vastly stunning. He had seen beauty in small proportions, in a figure or a person, but never in an area of land that encompassed him. Mary was precise about one thing: he felt as though he was on another planet. Surely nothing on Earth could be this magnificent. Each hill was higher than the next, with sheep and deer scattered along the sheets of green.

"You coming, brother?" Dex had already gathered their things and was indicating to the hotel.

Rory tore himself away from what he believed must be a mirage to follow Dex and Alice into the modest building across the way.

The three of them, being broke, shared a room in the hotel. After much arguing over who should take the meager twin-sized bed (Dex and Alice insisted Rory take it, whereas Rory insisted they have it to themselves), Rory climbed into the bed and almost immediately passed out. Dex and Alice curled up in the sleeping bags that they had packed and kipped on the floor, Alice enveloped in Dex's arms.

At 6 am sharp, Dex's phone alarm went off, waking Alice and himself with a start. She rolled over to turn away from Dex.

"Five more minutes," she mumbled groggily.

"Can't, love," Dex replied. "Today's the day."

Alice's eyes flew wide open. She turned back to face her beau, muttering one word. "Rory."

The two of them scrambled up, untangling themselves from the cocoons of their sleeping bags. Alice patted Rory's arm. "Wake up, Ror. It's Highlands Day!" Rory didn't stir. Dex began getting dressed, opening the curtains to let light in.

"Come on, Ror. It's time to get up," Alice repeated. "We've got a schedule to stick to if we want to make it before sundown this evening." But still, Rory made no effort to move.

Alice suddenly began to panic. She pressed her index and middle fingers to his carotid artery, attempting, desperate to feel a pulse.

Suddenly Rory jerked awake, sitting up straight and coughing. "What the bloody hell are you doing?" he yelled.

"I'm sorry!" Alice cried. "I'm sorry, you weren't moving so I just—-I don't know, I wanted to make sure you were breathing!"

"You don't press that hard, Alice, you cut off the circulation. Then I really will be dead!"

Dex, who hadn't paused since starting to get dressed, began to laugh.

"It's not funny, Dex!" Alice whined.

"It kind of is, Al," Dex chuckled. Rory began to laugh as well.

"Ugh, you two are such cocks sometimes," Alice said.

"Ah, yes, my girlfriend is such a classy lady, isn't she, Rory?" Dex said, smiling.

"Indeed she is. In fact, I don't think I've ever met anyone as posh as our Alice here."

Alice picked up the shoe that was closest to her and threw it at Dex, hitting him straight in the arm.

"Ow!" He clutched his elbow.

Since they would be driving to the starting point of their hike, they put their gear in the car and left the hotel. Dex carried the backpack containing the necessities: granola bars, water, morphine, and so on. He was hoping the whole time that they would not have to use the morphine — this would make the climb a much heavier one for Dex, as he would be the one carrying Rory.

They reached the foot of the Lost Valley, the portion of Glen Coe that they would be climbing, after driving for several miles in silence. The friends were relieved to find that several other groups of people had gathered in the car park and were preparing for a similar journey to theirs. They looked up at the brooding view of Glen Coe. The greenery that painted the entire landscape was so different from the bustling life of the city, and it was something that took some adjustment.

Dex adjusted the straps of his pack and looked at the others.

"It's not too late to back out, you know," Dex said, mainly to Rory.

Rory didn't say a word but began walking ahead of the other two.

"I guess that settles that then," Alice smiled. Dex nodded and placed his hand on Alice's back, guiding her ahead of himself.

The three mile hill walk that the three of them were going on should not have taken more than two hours, three at most. However, it was not long before every single person that they had seen in the car park had passed them. Within the first ten minutes, Rory had to stop and sit down on a rock to catch his breath.

"The air is much thinner up here than I anticipated," Rory conceded, waving away a concerned Alice who had rushed to his side.

After thirty minutes, Rory was heaving off the side of the hill. He was on all fours, and Dex was attempting to get him to drink water from the bottle he had brought. Rory refused, but Dex kept insisting.

"You're just making yourself dehydrated, Ror. The reason you're vomiting is that your body cannot physically handle this sort of stress. It needs to be replenished."

"Every bone in my body hurts," Rory grunted.

Dex reluctantly opened the bottle of liquid morphine. Rory took it from him and took a swig. He took a deep breath, then heaved himself up to his feet. "I'm alright."

Alice glared at him. "That would be a lot more believable if you hadn't just nearly passed out. Seriously, Rory, your body cannot handle this amount of exertion."

"I said I'm fine!" Rory yelled angrily, and began to limp up the rest of the hill. Dex knew that limp. It was the same one he noticed before anyone else did. Before his mother took Rory to the doctor.

When he had accused his brother of faking it for attention.

An hour went by, and the friends had only made it a little less than a mile. They came across a narrow path, and saw that there was no way through but to scramble across the rocks. Dex went first, followed by Rory. Alice spotted him the entire time. Rory had lost so much weight in just the last few months that he and Alice were almost the same size now. She helped lower his crippled body to Dex, who caught him just above the solid ground. Alice scrambled down the side quickly after.

The journey went like this for the majority of the time. Rory was quickly becoming drained and was making mistakes with where he planted his feet. This was making it difficult for Dex and

Alice to help him, as Dex had the pack and Alice was almost as tired as Rory.

Three hours later, the trio found themselves in the deepest groove of the valley, and in front of them was a sight that neither of them could have dreamt up in their minds.

They had found the Lost Valley, and they marveled in the mixture of colors that swirled together to fill the landscape. No longer was it pure green, but rather red, purple, green, yellow, and brown, all starting on the ground and spreading in opposite directions up the hills.

Close by was a smaller hill that they were able to climb up, to see perfectly just how high up they were from level ground, but also the magnitude of the mountains towering over them. Trapped in the middle by beauty.

Rory was suddenly overcome with great emotion. Like something was filling him up from the inside and about to burst out of him. He let the tears flow freely. Who cared if Dex or Alice saw him crying; what did it matter now? He had made it. He did something he assumed impossible, and he felt alive. More alive than he ever thought possible. And then all of the feelings swept over him at once: guilt, pleasure, heartache, love, regret, and hopefulness. How was it possible to feel so many things at once? Rory wondered. And then something else bubbled up inside of him and spilled over. The laugh came out more like a roar, and before he knew it, he was laughing and crying at the same time, and Dex and Alice were staring at him, speechless.

Rory continued to moan with grief and cry out with delight for several more minutes, before doubling over to catch his breath. He couldn't explain it. He was filled with so much agony that the love of his life would never experience this too, yet so joyful at the prospect that he was taking in something so fresh, so real, so beautiful.

Soon after Rory had regained his composure, he chuckled quietly. "I'm alright," he said breathlessly to Alice and Dex. Both had knelt down next to him, not sure whether to be concerned or laugh along with him. "I'm okay," he repeated, more trying to convince himself rather than comfort his friends.

No one said anything for several minutes. Neither Alice nor Dex could think of anything to say to Rory that wasn't already totally obvious. Sure, they could offer encouraging words like,

"Mary would be so proud," but some things don't need to be said to be communicated. The fact that his two favourite people left in the world were sitting next to him on the edge of this cliff meant more to Rory than anything else.

Even after several minutes of deep, controlled inhalations and exhalations, Rory couldn't seem to catch his breath. His heart felt like it was working in overdrive merely to get the poorly oxygenated blood to his brain. Everything swam before his eyes, and he shifted his weight to one of his hands to steady himself before it all came rushing back into view.

Dex put a hand on Rory's shoulder. "You alright, mate?"

Rory nodded. "Never better." And he smiled.

Dex and Alice began unpacking the picnic they had made from the pack, while Rory rested on the ground. They moved away from their friend, giving him space to be alone.

"You know," said Dex, "I was worried about Rory for certain. But I would have never pegged you as one for hillwalking."

"Are you joking?" Alice said. "My dad took me hiking all the time as a kid. "He and I would rough it just for the fun of getting out in nature."

"Seriously?" Dex said.

"I suppose there's a lot you don't know about me," Alice smiled as she opened a blanket and spread it out on the ground.

Rory pulled a fleece blanket out of his knapsack. He wrapped it around himself, just as a gust of wind nearly knocked him over. The sun was just starting to set, and he didn't want to run out of sunlight before it was too late. He dug around for some paper and a pen he had packed. Having found them, he flattened the paper on the rocky surface he sat on, shaking uncontrollably as he did so. He bent over the paper and began to write.

"You know, I suppose you're right," Dex conceded to Alice.

"About what?" she asked, as she unwrapped the cheese sandwiches she had made.

"About there being more to you than what I already know," Dex replied. "Maybe there's more to both of us than either of us know," he continued.

Alice laughed. "How do you mean?"

Dex was grinning uncontrollably now. He knew he looked foolish, but he couldn't help it. His heart began pounding, and he could feel his forehead beginning to sweat.

Rory etched out the last words he could get onto the paper. He fumbled as he folded it and secured it in his coat pocket. He closed his eyes and focused on his breathing. The burning in his left leg radiated all the way to his chest. He hoped his writing was legible. He could barely read his own words, his eyes were watering so much from the cold. The dry, thin air was suffocating his lungs, which were still having trouble getting the oxygen to his brain. He saw the green mountains across the way swim before him. He coughed and choked on the thick saliva stuck in his throat. He spat on the ground and took three long, shallow breaths.

Alice stared at Dex. "What are you saying, Dex?"

Dex moved closer to her and took her hand. "I'm saying that the last few years with you have been the best of my entire life. And that if I love you this much now, only time will tell how much more there is to love about you in the years to come."

Alice squeezed Dex's hand tightly, unable to control the beaming grin that began spreading across her face. Dex continued his soliloquy. "The past few weeks with Rory and Mary's letters have been...surreal. And it's shown me the depth of your heart that I know you only reserve for the people you care most about. One of those is me, I know. And the other is Rory. The fact that you would care so much for not only me but my own loved ones shows me what kind of woman you are. And you are the woman I want to share every happy moment, and every tragedy with. The woman I want to walk through life with. The woman whom I want to wake up next to every single morning for the rest of

my life. You are my One, Alice. You always have been. And with your acceptance—-" he pulled out the little black box that had been making a slight bulge in the pocket of his cargo pants and opened it—- "you always will be. And I will spend every day trying to live up to the man you deserve to have as your One."

Alice's mouth made a silent "O." She raised her hand to cover it but could not suppress the high-pitched squeal that escaped from it. "Yes!" she screamed. "Yes, yes, yes!"

Dex took the solitaire 14 karat gold diamond ring out of its case and placed it on Alice's left-hand ring finger. He looked into her eyes and held her gaze for several seconds before taking her in his arms and locking his lips with her own.

Alice's scream jolted Rory. He had assumed that she saw an insect, or that she had gotten a splinter or something. But when he saw Dex placing the ring on her finger, he knew the reality of the situation. Rory smiled. All was as it should be, he thought. He wanted to let his best friends share the joyful moment by themselves; he would congratulate them later.

He turned back around to face the open greenery. He took another breath in as deep as he could manage. He felt dizzy and placed a hand on the ground to steady himself. His heart began pounding twice the speed it had just a minute ago. The shooting pain in his leg was now felt throughout every inch of his body. He wanted his morphine, but it was in Dex's pack twenty feet away from him. He attempted to call out to Dex or Alice, but he choked on his words. He leaned further on the ground on his elbow now, gasping for air. His chest felt as though it was being stabbed by a million knives. He closed his eyes and prayed to black out, to not feel any more. He gained control of his breathing, and finally he was able to wrench his eyes open, determined not to miss the beauty that Mary wished upon his life. He then glanced back at his brother and Alice.

They would be alright, he thought. Even though the chilled air cut through his coat like ice, he suddenly felt warm. There was a heat in his abdomen that wasn't there before. This was not a feeling he was familiar with. It was a comfort he couldn't put a name to. Something he thought was surely only possible by some sort of miracle. And finally, he understood the feeling Mary had been trying to pass along to him since they met. The protection she chose while he chose fear. Finally, he recognized it. It was peace.

Epilogue

Dear Mary,

What a whirlwind these past few months have been. I thought that mourning your death would be the hardest thing I would ever do. And while this has been the worst past couple of months, I have also lived more and felt deeper than I ever have before. I have never been challenged before like I have these past weeks. And you did that to me, Mary. You did that *for* me.

I'm writing this from the best view second to looking at you. The Highlands in Scotland. Mary, I wish more than anything I could have told you these three words when you were still here. And no, it's not "I love you." You heard that more times a day than you probably would have liked. I wish I could go back in time and tell you: You were right. I kept you from experiencing life in fear of you dying sooner than you absolutely had to. And I am so sorry.

But that is not the sole purpose of this letter. Mary, I wish I could thank you. Thank you for opening my eyes to your world. You were my world, and I thought that I was yours. And I was jealous that you always put God before me. I think you would be proud of me for realizing this about myself.

I have finally understood your reason for trusting in something you cannot see. I see how I let my love for you define me, but you were able to find something bigger than either of us in which you found identity. And I suppose that is what made us so different. Even during the last days, with the depression and the physical hell you went through, you weren't resentful or angry. I will never get back the days I spent wallowing in my own self-pity and bitterness, but I can look forward to the days ahead. And while, here on Earth, those days are numbered, I know that something else lies ahead that will fill me with more joy than anyone, healthy or ill, will experience on Earth. And if that place for me is the same place you are, then that is just icing on this mixed emotions of a cake.

Know this Mary: You are the love of my life. And I will forever be grateful for how you were here for me even after your death. This is not the end, Mary. My spirit was crushed, long before you passed. I haven't healed completely, but one day I will.

Save me a place among the galaxies.

Your Rory

Acknowledgements

Thank you to Jonathan, Brennan, and Lynn, for being my first readers. Thank you to Liz, Chelsea, Emily, and Taylor, for listening to me read the very first drafts out loud in our dorm rooms at school when we should have been studying. I would also like to thank my wonderful editor from across the pond, Melanie Scott, for ensuring authenticity of the British dialogue and setting.

Finally, thank *you*, for taking a chance on these characters and their stories.

About the Author

Morgan Lima is a homegrown native to Nashville, Tennessee. She is a registered nurse, a lover of all things Broadway and British, and lives with her husband in Nashville. This is her first full-length novel.